DISCOVERY

DISCOVERY

Richard Neil LaBute Jr

ISBN: 978-1-959483-59-5 (sc)
ISBN: 978-1-959483-60-1 (e)

Library of Congress Control Number: 2023907864

DEDICATION

My brother Neil is the renowned half of our sibling duo. He has made his mark in the literary world with; 1) Screenplays, 2) Directing, 3) Stage Plays and 4) Production. This is his life and source of sustenance. He never seems to put down his pen and leave his mind to rest.

Although we have not been close over the years, I have followed his career and writing to some extent. In doing so, he must have had a part in awakening in me a desire to create, re-tell and share stories with others, of this I am certain.

In gratitude for his subtle nudging and dimly marked literary pathway, I thank him for being who he is and to him dedicate this story.

FOREWORD

With certainty, I can say, there have been written dozens of books related to the Lewis & Clark Expedition and the Louisiana Purchase. So why then have I chosen to join an already "crowded field", so uncharacteristic of me?

This short novel examines what it might have been like to be one of the players in this historical drama, from; 1) from Francois D-T Louverture – believing that the French Revolutionary slogan of Liberte, Egalite et Fraternite was inclusive of Negros of any social strata, 2) to Francois Barbe-Marbois – servant of France, but confusingly, which France? 3) to General Napoleon Boneparte short of cash and disposing of the Bourbon's non-producing colonial assets, 4) to the ever curious, and brilliant mind of President Thomas Jefferson, 5) to the talented, morose and ultimately suicidal Meriwether Lewis and 6) to the young, captive Shoshoni woman, Sacagawea, whose knowledge and soft-skills did so much to contribute to the success of the Corps of Discovery and to shape the nascent and manifest United States of America. Still other lesser characters in the story, real and composite played oversized roles in the creation of our historical story.

I believe therefore, the retelling of this grand adventure is a worthwhile effort and will excite its readers to always look beyond the headline event toward the human role in it.

Please remember, this story is a fictional telling which highlights historical persons, events and timelines. Other characters are composite or created.

Chapter 1

DISCOVERY

Francois-Dominique Toussaint Louverture appears resplendent in his martial regalia and finery as he arrives before French Divisional General Jean-Baptiste Brunet at an occupied plantation house near Cap-Francais in the French colony of Saint Domingue, island of Hispanola.

He has been invited by Monsieur *Le General* to *parley* in an effort to end the bloody Haitian Revolt, which has already killed or maimed thousands upon thousands of French *habitants*, soldiers and Haitians since the insurrection began in 1791. Unsuspecting, trusting a supposed peer, he arrives disadvantaged, without a strong bodyguard or route of escape. General Brunet finds the entire matter of pretense, deception and arrest unappealing to a gentleman such as himself. He curses General Leclerc under his breath for giving such an order. He then turns to a subordinate captain. "When the black bastard enters the portico, have the Corporal of the Guard disarm and arrest him. You have my permission to shoot his man guard out of hand.

They are treasonous filth, as is he. Cast him in irons and have him taken out to Admiral Joyeuse aboard the flagship *Ocean.* I don't want to have to deal with any escape attempts. He can rot out there in the hold of the frigate *Creole* until we decide what to do with him." *"A vos orderes mon general"*, replies the captain smartly as he turns to go organize the entrapment.

Louverture has unwisely pricked all the empirical players in the game. Learning first from the French, then working with the Spanish, English, then French again as empires, wars and revolutions rapidly change the rules. He prematurely announces himself Governor General For Life of Sainte Domingue, a colony within the auspices of the French Empire. This veil of subservience to the French Empire is a bit too thin for Emperor to be Napoleon and he orders his brother-in-law General Leclerc to arrest this upstart, *negre hautain*.

The recently incarcerated Governor for Life of Sainte Domingue does not live long enough to see the final French defeat. Under General Leclerc, the black, mulatto and mixed-race officers & men are stricken from the ranks of the army as unreliable. Soon thereafter, a yellow fever epidemic decimates the desertion-stricken French Army leaving it with 20 dead general officers including Leclerc, leaving only a few thousand soldiers still able to fight. Leclerc's successor, Divisional General Rochambeau is then defeated and later repatriated to France only after having spent some time as a "guest" of the British Royal Navy. As Louverture rots, not on the frigate *Creole*, but in a dank French prison castle of Fort de Joux on the French-Swiss border he succumbs to neglect, malnutrition and pneumonia in 1802, as his betrayer and fellow insurrectionist Jean-Jacques Dessalines becomes first President, then Emperor of the independent State of Haiti, until he too is betrayed and removed by assassination in 1806.

Notes: 1) *parely*, Fr. Informal negotiations, 2) *habitants*, Fr. colonists, 3) *a vos orderes mon general*, Fr. aye aye, sir

Monsieur Francois Barbe-Marbois is a cat of many lives. Dispatched to the fledgling United States as senior member of the French Legation under the *Ancien Regime*, he is popular with his American hosts, elected Honorary Foreign member to the recently founded American Academy of Arts and Sciences, corresponding with the governors of all thirteen colonies and even marrying an American, Elizabeth Moore, the daughter of the former governor of Pennsylvania.

Still as a member of Louis' bureaucracy, he becomes *intendant* for the colony of Sainte Domingue. "Lizzie, I know, as an American, you may not understand my motivations. Royalist or revolutionary, I am still French. I must go back to France and offer myself to her service, Elizabeth considers what could be a decision between life and death. Rumors abound as to the horrors occurring in revolutionary France. The rallying cry of *Liberte, Egalite et Fraternite* resounds with profound morality, but the reality of dispossession, arrest and death are real and frightening. "I am with you Francois, in this world and the next. Let us seek our destiny together," Elizabeth's lips quivering as she bravely utters the words. The year is 1789 as Francois and Elizabeth prepare for this journey, east, across the Atlantic to a new, Republican France much unlike France of the 900 year old house of the Bourbon he left only a few years before.

Notes: 4) *negre hautain*, fr. uppity nigger, 5) *Ancien Regime*, fr. referring to the Bourbon dynasty, 6) *intendant*, fr. bureaucratic official managing a department or region.

Preparing what possessions can be taken and what must be left, anxiety weighs heavily upon them both. "We shall not return in an official status, nor shall we embark upon a French vessel. Placing ourselves at whim of a ship's captain, be he *Feuillant, Jacobin,* or even a secret Royalist our freedoms may be jeopardized. We shall seek a cabin aboard a Dutch trading *fluyt* out of New York, take a passage to Rotterdam, then find our way home from there." Exclaims Francois, talking out loud but generally to Lizzie. She is half-listening, engrossed in her own thoughts and fears. She had sometimes fantasized about visiting France as the wife of a senior French diplomat to the French court, but never had she considered illegally entering revolutionary France *ex-officio*, suspect royalist of the *ancien regime.* "Lizzie, now remember. You must not tell our friends, even your confidantes, how we are returning to France. Only say, we are recalled on official business. We can explain ourselves later, when the present danger is past," instructs Francois.

"There, that's the last of it. 1 trunk each for personal items, a small, sealed chest for my papers, coin & your jewelry, and a handbag each. The coach leaves mid-afternoon, we'll arrive in New York tomorrow." Says Francois as he exhales. "I hear there is a new fluyt, just launched returning to the continent, The Hector. I'll try to get a cabin aboard her". New would be nice!"

"Yes, so nice my dear. I have enough trepidations about the cold, dark sea and stealing our entry into France. Fewer worries about a creaky old ship would be nice", replies Lizzie.

Notes: 7) *Liberte, Egalite et Fraternite,* Fr. motto of the French Revolution – Liberty, Equality and Brotherhood, 8) *fluyt,* Dutch. Type of sea-going cargo vessel, 9) *ex-officio,* Latin – out of duty, 9) *Feuillant, Jacobin,* Fr. – radical republican, or constitutional monarchy Jacobin

The journey to New York aboard Pease's Line is punctuated by jolts and stops. The ride aboard the stage wagon is not particularly comfortable, but today the wagon has only four paying customers, not the eleven it is designed to carry. The stage's team of horses enjoy the lighter burden and hurries along the rutted route. Good progress is made and nearing 7 p.m. the coach teamster blows his horn and stage pulls into a large, half-circle yard where it stops in front of an inn, Finnegan's Angry Goat.

"Peculiar name isn't it my dear? Scot-Irish no doubt, they have a very strange sense of humor! Remarks Francois. Let us debark. I doubt the "goat" serves wine, I shall have to make due with ale, but even ale sounds good to me right now." So, ale it is, Finnegan's Irish chowder and soda bread. No complaint is heard as the couple settles into a restful night. Early in the morning a breakfast is served. The teamster's horn seems loud, piercing the tranquility of the morning.

The team is already hitched and they and their teamster are anxious to complete the run to New York City. Everyone is rushed.

Time passes slowly at sea. The monotony is punctuated only by weather, of course, which is on the mind of every living soul, save perhaps the rodents busying themselves in the hidden places gnawing, scavenging and hiding. Losing reference to distance and geography, one's awareness rises and falls with each succeeding wave and the horizon beyond. Francois and Elizabeth count the days, knowing that a twenty-one day passage is the best outcome, yet a slow twenty-nine day voyage is just as likely. Reading, preparing some writing, and playing cards occupy their time. They share the meal table with the other passengers as not to provoke gossip, but spend most of the crossing together in their cabin, avoiding the others as much as is practical and possible.

Note: 10) Levi Pease started one of the first stage wagon lines in 1783. He was truly a transportation innovator expanding, merging, collaborating with 26 other lines to form a land transportation network in New England (primarily Boston, Hartford to New York

To Elizabeth, the dark dream of packing a few possessions, and an unpredictable cross-Atlantic voyage nears its end as the *fluyt* leaves the North Sea and glides past Hoek van Holland into the canal-like stream that bisects Rotterdam. In quaint, outlying villages, centuries-old churches stand stark against newly-built mansions on lands previously owned by noble lords who wrongly sided with the Spanish in the late war of Spanish Succession? Closer to the city but outside its walls, industries of the nuevo-rich, processors of sugar, tobacco, coffee and gin.

The ancient walls themselves struggle to contain houses, businesses, factories and warehouses, competing for every inch of space. Commerce seems to be on the lips of every citizen, be he or she rich or poor, mighty or marginalized. The *fluyt* ends this journey as Francois and Elizabeth disembark, having returned to a changing Old World.

CHAPTER 2

THE RETURN TO AN OLD WORLD

The busy docks, and bustling crowds of Rotterdam give the harried couple some respite from the feeling of being observed and discussed. Out of the city, the tranquil gentleness of pastoral countryside of the Netherlands and Luxembourg further calm their emotions for the days ahead. Metz, a northeastern city in the Lorraine region, disputed between Prussia and France, Metz is their destination.

"I spent many years in Paris, then later in Versailles forming myself in education, gaining confidence in the circles of influential men in order to groom my image at court, a court that no longer exists. Let us not despair, Lizzie, we shall return to Metz, the place of my birth, and my family and friends. Here we will be protected until I can divine the winds of politics and reintroduce "us" to those people who matter now." Muses Francois. "And if we are betrayed?

What then?" Questions Elizabeth. "Betrayal is ever present, even in times of normalcy.

Certainly, we must guard against it, plan our moves, but really all is in the hands of God, and God would, no doubt, advise us to scamper back across the border to the Grand Duchy of Luxembourg, I should think."

He laughs as the tension of the moment is broken. "My sister Jeanne, you know like Jeanne d' Arc, the maiden of Lorraine. She lives in Thionville, on the River Moselle, just north of Metz. I will contact her and find us some comfortable accommodations while I check for old colleagues and study the politics of Metz. Do you enjoy boats, my dear? I think that a small boat following the river to a quiet landing just outside Thionville would be a most inconspicuous arrival in France. The Moselle is renowned for its beauty, you know", exclaims Francois. "If you say so, dear", agrees Elizabeth half-heartedly.

The physical distance from Dudelange, near the Luxembourg frontier to Cattenom, France is less than 20 miles, then a further 10 miles south along the River Moselle to Thionville, where Francois' sister Jeanne, had lived, until now, a quiet life, far from the intrigues of Versailles and the upheaval in Paris. Here everyone expects Louis to return to the throne, perhaps tempered by demands of the *Estates General*. Little did they realize or know that already the Third Estate, that is, the common people, often led by lower hierarchy parish priests and country lawyers, had swept away feudalism and with, it old rules, taxation, and privileges.

The Third Estate had formed a new National Assembly, a revolutionary order, that of *Liberte, Egalitie, et Fraternite*, but in doing so making the old order of royalty, nobility and church princes, now enemies of the people.

After dark, on a shadowy October night, dogs bark followed by a light tapping on the back door of Jeanne's house. Frightened, she calls for her son, who proceeds to answer the door with barbed wrought iron poker in hand and his mother, holding a lamp stands behind.

Notes: 11) *Estates General* – a neglected legislative body in the ancient regime consisting of the First Estate (nobles), Second Estate (church princes), Third Estate (commoners). Dissolved in August 1789 in favor of a National Assembly, 12) *Qu'est-ce?* Fr. Who is it?, 13) *Si'l vous plait?*, Fr. Please, 14) *Bien sur, entrée, entrée*, Fr., But of course, come in, come in.

"Qu'est-ce?" "A friend. Please allow me in. I have news." Whispers a man's voice. "We are expecting no news." The boy replies. *"Si'l vous plait.",* Pleads the voice. The door swings open.

A darkly clad young man enters, nervously looking behind him as the door closes. *"Qu'est-ce?* I do not know you asks the boy once again. "I come on behalf of Francois." Says the young man.

"Francois? blurts out Jeanne. Why he is in America". "No, he is here." Assures the young man.

"He has come to see you. Will you accept his calling?" Asks the young man. "His wife also?

Bien sur, entrée, entrée.

With dark, hooded cloaks wrapped tight, two figures emerge from the backyard garden and quickly enter the house. The young man follows some minutes later with two trunks and a chest. Francois pays the young man in gold, a Dutch 10 guilder coin, almost twice a week's wage for a laborer. A smile of satisfaction breaks out across the young man's face as his hand clutches the coin, turns and disappears into the night.

"Oh brother, how, why do you suddenly appear here without even a letter, like the proverbial thief in the night?", exclaims Jeanne. "We could not risk being found out. Certainly, a letter from outside of the country would minimally provoke curiosity, would it not? Some nosey postmaster may very well have read the letter before you", explains Francois. "We did not know for certain the actual state of the country." "Nor do we, replies Jeanne. Many changes are said to have happened at Versailles or in Paris, but here nothing much is evident other than the *tricolore* cockade of the soldiers or the *bonnet rouge* worn by some in the streets, brother."

"A voila, this is why I chose to come here first, quiet, provincial Lorraine, other than to see the adorable face of my sister, of course", says Francois. "you are a good bureaucrat I am sure Francois. You never could tell the truth!" "Ah yes, the truth. What is truth? Is truth natural law, is truth the world as we, ourselves, see it? Or is truth that which was written

in stone so many millennia ago, shattered and never seen again? My truth is that of Decartes, *Je pense, donc je suis*, counters Francois. So, dear sister, we are here. First enlighten me with all the news of our extended family, then tell me what you can about our new France, every detail you can think of."

The young man with the bright gold Guilder in his pocket rows at a measured, steady pace following the north flowing current of the Moselle back toward Cattenom. The darkness casts a protective shadow over him and his boat. He is giddy about his prospects with the coin. On this return trip however, the young man and his boat do not go unnoticed. He is followed as he runs the skiff ashore and hurries for home. Betraying his residence in the act of opening the front gate, he freezes as a voice breaks the stillness of the pre-dawn hour. *"Arrete, si'l vous plait!"*, orders a *gendarme*. "Who are you?" asks the young man. "No, I ask the questions, you provide me with answers, responds a voice with patient force. Truthful answers, of course. It is simpler that way. Now, what is your name?" "Etienne. My name is Etienne LeBlanc", answers the young man. *"Bien.* Now Etienne LeBlanc, why are you out so late or so early, hurrying home from such a pleasant time on a dangerous river in the dark? Fishing perhaps? But you have no fish! Carrying something somewhere? Maybe, but this is not evident, yet. Tell me, simply, what are you, what were you doing?" questions the *gendarme* again. Etienne, hesitates, for no clever answer finds its way to his lips. He stands there in silence, a loaded silence that sheds light on the gendarme's suspicions. "Oh, I see. You do not know why you are up so early, or so late, or what you were doing on a boat on a dangerous river in the dark. No easy answers. I understand. That is why I am here, to find those answers.

Notes: 15) *tricolore*, Fr. blue, white, red colors of the Revolution, 16) *bonnet rouge*, Fr., red liberty bonnet of the Revolution, 17) *A voila*, Fr., there, you see, 18) *Je pense, donc je suis*, Fr., I think therefore I am (Rene Decartes 1637. *Cogito, ergo, sum*

But, you must be chilled. Why not come with me. We shall go to my place of work, have some hot coffee and search for these answers together I." "Am I arrested then?" blurts out Etienne. "Arrested? Why should I arrest you. Have you done something unlawful? No, I think not. I invite you to join me in a coffee. Of course, I am just a poor policeman, and have no sugar. But perhaps once you have warmed yourself, you will find it easier to answer my few questions, *n'est pas?*

In a small suite of rooms located within the modest city hall of Cattenom, Monsieur Le Gendarme and Etienne finish their coffee. "Now Etienne, my friend. You are my friend, *n'est pas?* Since you cannot tell me what you were doing, show me. Empty your pockets here on my table!" Etienne hesitantly complies with the order. His pockets are empty, save one, bright gold Guilder. *"Oh mon Dieu,* my new found friend is a surprisingly rich man. Now tell me once more, how is it that a young man from the village of Cattenom, modestly dressed, out in the late hours of the night, alone, on a boat, on a dangerous river should come to have such a large sum of money in his pocket. And foreign money at that. What have you been doing, Monsieur Etienne? "Running away, sir. I was running away", blurts out Etienne. "Running away? From whom? To where? No clothes, no food. *Non,* I do not think so. I think perhaps you were, for lack of a better word, smuggling something, somewhere, for which you were handsomely paid.

Sugar perhaps? No, you would have kept a small quantity in your pocket, as would have I, for our coffee. I think maybe you were smuggling someone or something that does not wish to be seen in the light of the day? What were you doing, Etienne? I will find out you know. Simply tell me now and it go easier for you. Perhaps I'll even return your newly acquired gold Guilder.

Notes: 18) *Arrete, s'il vous plait,* Fr., stop please, 19) *gendarme,* Fr., policeman, 20) *Bien,* Fr., good

Etienne quickly calculates his diminishing odds of escaping the clutches of this strangely clever policeman. He deeply desires to retrain his night's earnings, so decides to chance a partial, untraceable truth. "Yes, sir. It is true. I did ferry two persons from Cattenom to a landing just north of Thionville. I do not know where they went from there," Etienne lies. "Certainly, no questions asked, no talking, no names, but someone knows something and it's that something that we, Inspector Jean-Claude Forneau and Etienne, are going to discover—together. You may go home now. I will keep your little treasure as security. Report back to me tomorrow. We shall pay a visit to Thionville, if for no other reason to visit with my colleague there. *Bon Soir*, Etienne. Don't think too much on this matter or on running away from home.

That would disappoint me greatly. *A bien tot"*, concludes Forneau.

As ordered, Etienne presents himself to the Inspector at the City Hall office the next morning at 1000. "My compliments Etienne, you have kept our appointment. Now let us board that skiff of yours and retrace your journey – to that landing just north of the Thionville." Time passes slowly as Etienne tacks against the current, south toward Thionville. "Where now exactly did you go ashore, my friend?" queries Forneau. "I cannot exactly say, sir. It was dark and I was ordered by my passenger to turn in", mumbles Etienne without conviction. "Ah, as I expected. You are not sure. So, let us put in at the village pier. Perhaps someone there can recall seeing such a fine, little craft as this? What was the time again, an hour past midnight? two?"

Notes: 21) *N'est pas,* Fr., Isn't that right?, 22) *O mon Dieu,* Fr., Oh, my God, 23) *non,* Fr., no

Inspector Forneau is disappointed to learn that the village watchman seems not to recall the skiff arriving or departing Thionville pier. He turns then to his fellow gendarme there, requesting information should anyone or anything odd come to his attention. "You know, my little friend here knows much more than he is willing to say. I will keep a close eye on him as well as withholding his, probably ill-gotten, treasure until I have satisfied myself with this case." confides Forneau to his fellow *gendarme* before taking leave. Walking toward the pier, Forneau observes his charge furtively glancing down a street. He notes, Rue Lazare Carnot. He then stops and turns back toward the city. "Go prepare your skiff. I will join you shortly", he informs Etienne. The boy goes to the pier as ordered while Forneau doubles back to the *Gendarmerie.*

"A hunch, my friend. Watch Rue Lazare Carnot. Something tells me.....", mentions Forneau to his fellow *gendarme.* He then departs for the pier and home.

"To be honest with you, my dear sister, Thionville is not our destination. I must find our way back to Metz where I can discuss, with trusted friends, the true state of affairs at Versailles and in Paris. I wish to offer my services and self to the National Assembly and to France, but cannot divulge my presence here until I am assured that we, Elizabeth and I, will be received without prejudice. It seems that functionaries of the *ancien regime* have fallen from favor", explains Francois.

"Yes, brother, everyone is under suspicion these days. Neighbor watches neighbor, *les gendarmes* and soldiers watch everyone. We are made to feel almost criminal for owning a small house with a garden." "Perhaps we could send your maid to Metz with a message?"

Francios interjects, "unwritten, of course." Suzette? Yes, that is possible. With a message?

Notes: 24) *Bon Soir,* Fr., good night, 25) *A bien tot,* Fr., see you soon,

Most certainly unwritten. I should not want her to be exposed in any way. You and Elizabeth stay here, out of sight, until she returns with your answer", proposes Jeanne. "Does she even know we are here? Who we are?" asks Francois. "Yes, she knows some persons arrived late last night. No, she does not yet know who you are", replies Jeanne thinking. "Let's keep it that way for now, sister. It is best for all concerned", adds Francois.

"Suzette, go to Metz, buy something there, then continue on to the university at Pont-a-Mousson. Ask for Professor Jacques DeBois. When he receives you, tell him only that Francois d'Amerique needs to meet with him at the earliest opportunity. Discretion is most important.

Let him choose the time and place – but soon! Now hurry", instructs Jeanne.

As Inspector Forneau waits and contemplates his next move, Suzette hurries to Metz and beyond. In Metz she strolls the market, then slips away following the road south to nearby Pont-a-Mousson and the university there. The distinguished professor DeBois, curiously receives the comely, young girl Suzette in his office study. Healthy men, often fantasize that young ladies might have more than the stated business on their minds. This would be a welcome distraction in the dark times of the new French Republic. Alas, no such whimsical fantasy for middle-aged Professor DeBois, only a cryptic message from an old friend and classmate via this flaxen-haired courier. Strange but not so strange given the times! DeBois orders a carriage be made ready post haste for a trip to Thionville. Suzette is offered a seat in the carriage with Professor DeBois, an offer which is readily accepted. He smiles.

Note: 26) *Gendarmerie,* Fr., police station

Comfortably seated in the carriage, professor DeBois and Suzette make quick progress on the main throughfare from Pont-a-Mousson to Metz. He queries her, as he offers her an exotic chocolate from a wicker basket of refreshments on the seat beside him. "So, Francois d'Ameriquie? When did he arrive? Is he alone?" "No, sir. He is not alone. A lady accompanies him. He arrived late, last night. I was sent to you after they had eaten breakfast this morning."

"Ah, I see." "Of course, he said nothing to you directly, did he?" "No sir, they did not speak to me. This sweet is delicious, sir." DeBois see an opportunity. He retrieves another delicacy from his basket, then leans toward the naïve maid as he presents his bribe, a chocolate in his left hand, his right hand softly placed on her knee. She flinches slightly but accepts the chocolate, directly from his hand to her mouth. She experiences a quiver of excitement as he deliberately continues to slide his right hand up her leg, pulling up her skirt with it and exposing first her stocking, then the smooth, white skin of her thigh. "Monsieur DeBois! she half-heartedly protests. You are a dishonorable man." "No, I am not, he protests. Only when confronted with such innocent beauty, my moral compass spins on its axis." She coos. The old professor and the young maiden fumble among the cushions of the carriage as it continues it journey north to Thionville. He first consummates the act with his finger, then later, as she recovers exhausted from the effort, he continues with the extension of a man's soul. Now, he too is exhausted. They sleep peacefully for the rest of the journey.

The coach arrives at 150, Rue Lazare Carnot, Thionville late. The arrival of the sleek, black carriage and handsome team, draws the attention of the gendarme even before the disheveled professor and maid-messenger enter the house. The policeman waits to see where the driver intends to refresh himself. Public houses are always a good source of information.

After discharging his fares, the carriage driver navigates the narrow streets of Thionville to a local livery stable. There he himself unharnesses his prize team and makes certain they are properly watered, fed and stabled. He then walks to a nearby inn, Le Barbe d'Or, where he quenches a powerful thirst with local ale followed by a meal of *saucisson d'Armagnac*, carrots and potatoes. Little does he know, nor does he suspect that from the shadows of the public room he is being observed by one who appears to be but another hungry traveler. The *gendarme* hurries back to send his message to Inspector Forneau in Cattenom.

"Old friend how are you?", opens DeBois as he is greeted by Francois. Suzette curtsies slightly before Jeanne then disappears to her room. "Jacques, so good to see you. I did not expect you to come here. I had thought that we might meet somewhere", states Francois slightly annoyed that the professor should so openly reveal his temporary lair. "No, no. When I was informed of your presence back on French soil, then asked to meet, I knew it was most important. I thought the best course of action was to come directly to you as soon as possible.

How may I serve you, old friend?" asks DeBois "The truth is, Jacques, I need to discreetly contact friendly members of the Assembly and reintroduce myself as a faithful servant of France, willing to serve. I fear that a more direct approach may fall to a hostile member, who may think of me as a royalist, a bureaucrat of the *ancien regime*, explains Francois. I brought Elizabeth with me, in spite of the dangers, because this process may take some time and we do not wish to be apart. Also, I thought her presence might demonstrate my sincerity in the matter."

Note: 27) *saucisson d'Armagnac*, Fr., sausage of duck & pork

"Sincere or not, one can't easily divine the machinations of Paris. First, the *Estates General* are overpowered by the Third Estate, which then declares a National Assembly. This Assembly, is for the moment, leaning toward a constitutional monarchy, but the king, his family and many of his entourage are arrested. Moreover, sinister elements control the back rooms of Paris, The Society of Jacobins. And even the Jacobins are divided between The Montagnards, and the Girondins. For the moment the Girondins hold sway, but beware of the Montagnards! Their leader is young, firebrand lawyer named Maximilien Robespierre, explains Jacques. You may have been wise to have remained in the New World, far away from the Old!"

Inspector Forneau believes his suspects to be firmly in the trap, exactly what crime or crimes his suspects have committed, he is still unsure. The local magistrate, trying to bolster his republican credentials, has, in advance, signed several warrants, providing the Inspector maximum flexibility in pursuing and arresting Forneau's would-be suspects. This process has taken longer than the Inspector had hoped, and he finds himself now rushing south to Thionville by horse.

"Let us leave here in the morning for Pont-a-Mousson. I will find comfortable lodging for you at the university guesthouse. I can also contact the Senior Magistrate in Metz and work-out what could become a border violation problem for you. I will tell him that you and Elizabeth are invited guests of the university. Entering and exiting the country has become a serious obstacle in recent months. The National Assembly doesn't want important players from the *ancien regime* escaping their grasp at least until some of these dubious accounts are settled.

I can imagine these formerly important persons being keen on departing post-haste, but even for the common folk carrying-on normal cross border commerce, it has been difficult. All of European nobility is connected someway, be it by blood, marriage or obligation. The Assembly, particularly these Jacobins, are paranoid about interference from outside of our borders. The peculiar aspect in your case however is that few are trying to smuggle themselves into France, so, just maybe, my Senior Magistrate colleague will see our request as being, less than nefarious?" outlines DeBois.

"Excellent. We have the makings of a plan then. To the morning and a spectacular carriage ride along the beautiful River Moselle", with good French cognac in hand, Francois toasts.

The Gendarme has collected no information other than the place of origin of the carriage.

Having left the inn late, he returns early and finds the teamster has already taken his breakfast, his team harnessed and hitched ready to go. He silently observes, following the teamster and the carriage to 150 Lazare Carnot Street, where he further notes 3 well-dressed persons boarding the conveyance with heavy luggage. Without delay the teamster whistles, then snaps his whip in the air and they depart, south along the river road, the road to Metz.

Later in the day, the Inspector arrives in Thionville. "*Mon Dieu* Citizen Inspector, what took you so long? I sent a message yesterday, laments the Gendarme. The persons of interest have already gone, departed earlier this morning, by carriage. Two middle-aged men, and a woman.

I can never guess the age of women, but I would guess she is the wife of one of the men. Very pretty, she is. They carry heavy luggage"

"And from where did these 3 depart?" asks the Inspector "150 Lazare Carnot Street, sir. The residence of Jeanne Canard", replies the Gendarme crisply. He is proud of having the requisite information at hand.

"*Bien*. Is it Miss Canard or Mrs. Canard?" asks the Inspector "Mrs Canard, Inspector. She is a widow. Then Canard is not her surname? Do you know her Maiden name? Where she comes from? Her family?" further queries the Inspector "Unfortunately, no, Inspector. I have only been posted here in Thionville a short time, since the revolution. I hail from Brittany", says the Gendarme.

"I really don't much care from whence you hail. I care only about where our suspects have gone and who they really are. A more complete answer to these pressing questions may be gotten from this Mrs. Canard. I will start there before pursuing the carriage further", states the Inspector. The two policemen proceed to 150 Lazare Carnot Street and knock on the door. Suzette answers the door.

"*Bon Jour*, Mrs. Canard?" greets the *gendarme* politely.

"No, sir. I am the housekeeper. Mrs. Canard is at home though. I will call her", responds Suzette.

"*Merci*. We will wait here", responds the *Gendarme* in kind. Suzette disappears into the house, and Jeanne comes to the door.

"Mrs. Canard"? again asks the *Gendarme*.

"Yes, it is I. How may I help you?" asks Jeanne maintaining a confident demeanor.

The Inspector takes charge of the conversation. "Mrs. Canard, I am Inspector Forneau. I wish to ask you about guests who may have called on you recently."

"Guests? You mean my brother? Has my brother done something of interest to the *Gendarmerie*? I think not", answers Jeanne pleasantly but with shortness.

"Your brother you say? And his name?"

"Francois Barbe-Marbois. Why do you ask?" answers Jeanne again with shortness "Barbe-Marbois? An old name? Is Barbe-Marbois your maiden name also."

"Yes."

"Where does your family come from, may I ask?"

"Historically, Lorraine, near Metz. Unless you have something pertinent to ask of me, I wish to entertain your query into my family heritage no longer. Good day, gentlemen." says Jeanne thereby terminating the conversation abruptly.

"Thank you, Mrs. Canard. We have no further questions, at this time. However, you should be aware that providing shelter and sustenance to a criminal is, in itself a crime.

"A criminal?"

"Yes, I suspect that your brother has crossed the frontier illegally, therefore, by law, a criminal, and you then, the same." warns the Inspector becoming suddenly almost threatening.

"I see. No, my brother, as I have told you is Francois Barbe-Marbois. Our family hails from Lorraine. We are French. He is not a criminal. Good day, gentlemen." concludes Jeanne with a hate-like threat in her eyes.

The Inspector mounts his horse, giving no further instructions to the Gendarme. He trots out at a determined pace for Metz.

The University carriage and its three passengers leisurely enters the old fortress city of Metz.

It is decided to disembark and take lunch at an inn while the horses rest and are watered. For Elizabeth, this is her first experience of true French cuisine although Lorrainian regional delicacies are often a fusion of German and French tastes. They enjoy authentic Lorrainian *Tete de Veau et Brioche Tressee* washed down with sweet Moselle wine.

"The veal was exceptional Professor DeBois. Being ethnically Dutch, I've always preferred *Dikke Koek,* a Dutch sweetbread. But the *Brioche Tressee* was delicious. American colonials seem to prefer more traditional English white or rye bread, but I do love the sweetbreads of Holland, now France. Thank you", exclaims Elizabeth.

Having spent a leisurely two hours dining in Metz, the three passengers take their places in the coach, and they continue south on the river road to Pont-a-Mousson, home of the university.

Notes: 28) *Tete au Veau,* Fr., Lorrainian veal specialty, 29) *Brioche Tressee,* Fr., Lorrainian sweetbread, 30) *Dikke Koek,* Dutch, Sweetbread with currants

The Inspector also breaks his journey at Metz. His horse is tired as is he. In spite of being an above average horseman, he is not used to longer rides at such a determined pace. He liveries his horse, then seeks at quiet place to rest himself for an hour or so. He eats, but avoids drinking but a bit of ale.

Returning to his horse and saddle, the Inspector continues at a walk through on the main road through the city. At the south end of the city, he notices a guard post, manned by soldiers, regulars of *L'Armee Revolutionnaire Francaise*, he is surprised. Stopping at the guard post, he identifies himself and asks for the Corporal or Sergeant of the Guard. After some minutes, an ill-tempered looking Sergeant appears.

"Citizen Sergeant, I am Chief Inspector Forneau." He exaggerates his actual standing in order to impress the Sergeant of the Guard into self-serving cooperation.

"Yes, Chief Inspector. How may I assist you?"

"I am in pursuit of a black carriage which may have passed your post. Three persons are aboard. One or more are suspected of having crossed the frontier illegally. Have you seen a carriage pass here this afternoon with three or more passengers aboard", questions the Inspector.

"Why yes, Chief Inspector. Not more than an hour ago, the carriage passed by here. It was halted and questioned. Three persons were aboard, one being a handsome lady. They are enroute to the university at Pont-a-Mousson", reported the Sergeant.

"Thank you, Sergeant. I am in pursuit", blurts out the Inspector as he kicks his mount into an canter.

After a thirty or forty minute ride, the Inspector sees, first dust, then obscurely the back of a black carriage. He pushes his mount forward, faster, ever faster. The horse, already tired from the long canter, begins to sweat profusely and snort. The riverlets of horse sweat spring forth from his chest following the contours of his neck back, disappearing into the mane. By now, even the horse's mane becomes wet enough to produce sweat droplets leaping into the air, splattering against the Inspectors clothes. Still he presses on. Within sight of the carriage, the teamster atop, the heads of passengers seen visibly swaying through the back window of the carriage, his horse falters, it trips on a pebble or the irregular road. First the right front leg, then the left, suddenly horse falls flat on its knees, then head over heels in a somersault. The beast breaks its neck in the tumble and lands squarely on top of the late Inspector Forneau, as the carriage rumbles on, completely unaware of the accident only a hundred feet to its rear.

Chapter 3

IN THE SERVICE OF
A REVOLUTION

Summer 1795

The time of our mere existence here in France has come to an end my dear Lizzie. I know that many things have been whispered and said about *Le Directoire,* in particular about Robespierre. Robespierre is dead and moldering in his grave without eternal hope. We are still alive and I am to be one of *Les Anciens,* in *Le Conseil Des Anciens.* We are the senior partners to *Le Conseil des Cinq-Cent.* Together, we rule all of France. It is unimaginable to me, to have lived and served the absolutism of the Bourbon, and now with a few hundred of my elected countrymen to be ruling France in their stead. Think of it, elected members", crows Francois.

"Yes my dear, it is so wonderful that your talents should be again recognized for what they are and that awful accusation that you had somehow been complicit in the death of the police inspector is behind us. I didn't know how much longer I could live here under that dark cloud of whispers and innuendo", confesses Elizabeth with relief.

"We can thank God for Professor DeBois and his connections with the Senior Magistrate of Metz. Without Jacques, I would, without doubt, be sharing meals with rats in some prison hole or worse, possibly, the national razor, *le guillotine.*

Elizabeth adds, "Since our arrival here in France, how many have met their fates on the scaffold of the guillotine? Thousands I think. *La Terreur* turned the country into a madness feasting on itself. The Committee of Public Safety is an oxymoron in its truest sense. I will never understand what happened around us. Only by the grace of God did we survive."

"It is true, Lizzie. But I cannot say without a measure of dishonesty that I am sorry to see some of those "princes of the Church" and blood-sucking titles with their heads in baskets or on pikes. Louis, was naïve and stupid. If he hadn't tried to run away into the arms of his Austrian in-laws, he and his family may well have still been alive today. That was the excuse the Committee was looking for. The Committee was looking for counter-revolution as a way to explain away its problems. Louis gave them counter-revolution by trying to save himself. He played right into their fears and hands. Louis is as responsible for the *La Terreur* as the Committee" Francois says with lament.

Much to Francois' disappointment, the years 1795-1797, Years III-V of the Revolution, prove to be difficult ones. The National Assembly, far from being a homogenous body, squabble, argue and fight. As the uncertainties of the Revolution drag on, more Assemblymen and their constituents look back nostalgically on the rich history and relative stability of the Bourbon.

Only a short while post- demise of Robespierre, *Le Directoire*, with the support of *L'Armee Revolutionaire Francaise* questions the guidance, even the loyalty of the National Assembly and charts an ever more radical and dictatorial course.

Notes: 31) *Le Directoire,* Fr., Five member Oligarchy which ruled France 1795-1799, 32) *Les Anciens,* Fr., The Elders, 33) *Le Conseil des Anciens,* Fr., Counsil of Elders or Upper House of the revolutionary French Assembly. 25members, 34) *La Terreur,* Fr., The Terror. Period 1793-1794 when the Committee for Public Safety led by M. Robespierre purged France of royalty, nobles, clergy and counter-revolutionaries

Buoyed by self-assuring peer support, Francois speaks his mind freely regarding the past, present and future. But Francois' free thoughts and words as well as those of others, run counter to *Liberte, Egalitie et Fraternite* as defined by *Le Directoire*. Spies are everywhere gathering facts, creating fiction as their partisanship and prejudices dictate. A dangerous world becomes increasingly dangerous in revolutionary France, a revolution that continues to gurgle, boil and consume.

"Lizzie, it is an impossible task! Robespierre *et Les Montagnards* may be gone, a few surviving *Girondins* restored, but *Le Directoire*, the oligarchy of five, are all elected from the *Le Conseil des Cinq-Cents* supported by *L'Armee Revolutionaire Francaise* which in turn is made-up of illiterate *Sans-Culottes*. *Les Anciens* prefer the ministries and bureaucracy controlled by gentleman, and persons of education. *Les Cinq-Cents* et *Les Sans-Culottes* are a half-educated, rabble seeking only revenge and creating anarchy. France can't go on year after year warring on its neighbors while ferreting out supporters of *Le Ancien Regime*, the clergy and emigres.

The economy is in shambles, inflation is high without any real money to be had, and we continue to involve ourselves in border disputes. What will become of France? It wasn't this bad under the worst days of Louis!" groans Francois.

"Francois, you mustn't despair! France, we, have already endured so much, it cannot possibly be to no end. But you must be careful. If you express such sentiments in public, surely someone will denounce you as a royalist", warns Elizabeth.

"I was just saying, it wasn't so bad under *Les Bourbons*. I'm not particularly a royalist, neither am I a committed revolutionary. I just want stability and peace for France.

"I know the intentions of your heart, Francois, but your loose words may get us both imprisoned or killed", warns Elizabeth.

"As usual, you are right, of course. I must not despair nor can I express any misgivings, to anyone. The danger is clear and present. But I do long for a simpler time, when we were younger and in America", reflects Francois.

Two years pass as Francois learns to navigate the intricacies of the balance of power in revolutionary France. It is not difficult for Francois to understand *Le Conseil des Anciens*, all men, over 40, educated and most having served the Bourbon in some manner. The sitting members of *Le Conseil des Cinq-Cents* however are a different matter. These citizen legislators are younger, come from a variety of backgrounds, with little or no experience, and are, for the most part, less educated. *Les Cinq-Cents* tend to be radical in their hatred of *le ancien regime.*

Years before, in 1790, the Assembly passed The Civil Constitution of the Clergy, a law, which in effect subordinated the French Roman Catholic Church to the state. Deacons, priests, bishops and so on were required to swear fealty to the French State, as monastic orders, both of men and women were abolished, and lands confiscated, so hated was the power of the Church.

Some clergy refused to comply with said Civil Constitution law. These men were tried, and sentenced to transport to French Guiana where they were forced into communal hard labor and re-education. In 1794, after the execution of Robespierre, some 193 Jacobins are sent to Guiana as political prisoners, most will die there of disease and despair. These events hang over Francois like a dark cloud, ever threatening.

Yet Francois, while tacking in the political winds, does not lose his "moral compass", as quoted by his close friend Professor DeBois, those many years ago. He supports those, who like him, were functionaries of *Le Ancien Regime* and who view a Constitutional Monarchy as a road to stability. In 1797, Francois is denounced in the Assembly.

Notes: 35) *Les Montagnards,* Fr., Radical faction of the Jacobins, strongly proletariat 36) *Les Girondins,* Fr., Moderate faction of the Jacobins, more bourgeois, 37) *Sans-Culotte,* Fr., literally without breeches. Commoners known to wear *pantaloons* (trousers) instead of the silk breeches then popular with the aristocracy.

"My dearest Elizabeth, how can I declare to you, I have been denounced within the Assembly as a royalist and counter-revolutionary. I have ruined our lives but I have not pimped our principals. I stand firmly in the belief of *Liberte, Egalite et Fraternite*, including those who served the Bourbons and those of us who believe constitutional monarchy to be in the best interests of all the citizens of France. Oh, can you ever forgive me? Bleats Francois.

Francois has been netted in the anti-royalist coup of September 1797. The outcome of his trial, and the terms of his sentence are foregone conclusions.

"It is the judgement of this court, that you shall be taken from this place to a lawful prison.

There you will await availability and passage on the next transport to the French Colonial Territory of Guiana in the Western Hemisphere. There you shall live and labor in commune.

Your sentence there shall not be less than five years, but may be greater should you fail to confess yourself to the ideals of the revolution. Your family, shall be declared *persona non grata* and deported from France. So says this court." Announces the presiding judge.

Chapter 4

EXILE

September 11, 1797

My dearest Elizabeth,

I find myself here, awash in the Atlantic, bound for a destination not of my choosing, but imposed upon me as sentence of a secular court for following my God-given conscience. Ah, God-given, a sentiment that enrages citizens of the revolution, who somehow believe that God is now subservient to the Republic of France! My words no doubt sound angry and bitter, as perhaps they are. I am angry and bitter at the prospect of being separated from you for these months or even years, only God knows.

I will endeavor to persevere as I know you will also. Our souls are forever bound together in this life and the next. I pray only for your health and wellbeing, and that, God willing, we will meet again soon.

We are generally not ill-treated as you might have imagined. The attitude of our jailers is something between prisoner and colonist. It is said that we are bound for Cayenne in Guiana. The heat of the equilateral regions do not give me pause for concern, but the abundance of tropical vapors and creatures do. I shall do my best to remain in good health and survive this trial by ordeal. God will not abandon me now.

Once we reach Cayenne, I will post this letter. Hopefully it will return quickly to France, or follow you wherever you have gone, I suspect back to your father's house in Philadelphia? They have not stripped us of our surnames, so you may write to me as; Citizen Colonist Francois Barbe-Marbois, Cayenne, French Guyana. I am certain that your letter will eventually find me, ever waiting.

Your loving husband,

Francois

The transport arrives in Cayenne as other transports before it. Once pier side, its involuntary citizen-colonists debark with a sack of meagre possessions. They wait, and wait, and wait in the oppressive heat. After a time, they are herded down a dusty avenue to a processing center, where it will be decided, where each man will be assigned. Each man is captive to his own thoughts and fears as they co-mingle, whisper with averted eyes and wait again. A ray of hope lightens Francois' face, as an orderly in colonial uniform collects the letters written by the men while aboard the transport. He assures the skeptical faces that the letters will be returned to France on the next vessel.

Assigned to Farm #4, Francois is transported by ox cart on one of the crude roadways built by previous Citizen-Colonists. This in itself is a hot, rough and unpleasant journey so unlike the wonderful carriage ride along the River Moselle, seemingly a lifetime ago.

Farm #4 is not so much an agricultural plot as an engineering project in the mind of some creator or more likely an ignorant bureaucrat looking at a map. A cluster of poor structures occupy at small clearing. Undergrowth is cut away, then giant hardwoods, drainage ditches, some small garden plots, and a grid patchwork of tillable parcels to be. Though bone tired at the end of the day, Francois turns to his pen.

January 22, 1798

My dearest Elizabeth,

Not knowing whether my last letter has even reached you, or for certain where you are or how you are, still my pen in the service of my love for you gives me solace. On meager rations, we work the daylight hours, toiling to create a farm, where no farm exists. Foliage cut away seems to regrow even stronger the next week. Huge hardwoods of mahogany and cypress jut out of the swampy soil toward the heavens, the soil saturated like a sponge. We are given some time at the end of the day to tend our gardens. Without these gardens we would surely starve to death. Our allotted ration is rice and tea, supplemented with whatever we can either forage or grow. Meager rations indeed.

Many of my fellow citizen-colonists are Jacobin transportees, although fewer and fewer of our host consist of this blight of humanity. Although I share their burden and suffering, they suffer less than they deserve. May God have mercy on their souls, if they even possess souls?

My will is strong but my hand grows weak as I am at the end of my day. I must rest and prepare my poor body for the morrow. With all my heart and soul, I send my love to you wherever you may be.

Your loving husband
Francois

Within weeks of his arrival on Farm #4, Francois' intelligence is recognized and he is reassigned from field laborer to assist in the management of the community.

Francois is given a small desk in the main administrative building of the commune. The building doubles as the superintendent's home leaving all available floorspace to be used in some fashion.

Superintendent Pierre Wagrez confides in his new-found friend. "The first group of transportees were those damned Jacobins. They are a weird lot. I half expected to wake up dead some morning. There is a look in their eyes, it's all same look, like they are staring right through you into another world. They live on the other side. Fortunately for me, most of the Jacobins have never worked an honest man's labor one day in their miserable lives. At the end of the day they were too tired to cause much trouble and settle down. They are, for the most part, fair-skinned, soft-palmed city boys. Many of their number have just curled up and died.

Sure, a snake bite here and there, a gator, some have tried to run off, they just disappear into the interior. I warned them on arrival to take advantage of what we offer here because there is no escape. The native Arawaks who inhabit the periphery of our civilization will shove a spear up your ass if they capture you, then roast and eat you. They are a frightening looking lot, the Arawaks. I've seen a young one or two that a man could fuck, but then put em right back in a cage."

"Qui, Monsieur Wagrez, I have seen it too. Even in my short time, the Jacobins, for whatever reasons, have not prospered here." Replies Francois seriously.

"Prospered!! Well, there's a politically correct word if I've ever heard one. Prospered! No, they are so busy either conspiring, resisting or just oblivious of the reality around them, they don't last long. It's really rather droll isn't it. It is the vapors, bugs and natives that are killing them, not us. If they would only accept their fate, work hard and confess their misguided ways, they could be promenading the Champs Elysees once again. As a group however, I suspect these "enlightened" leaders of the Revolution, will all die here in the bogs of Guyana, forgotten!"

"Transported and forgotten, like us." Quips Francois.

Chapter 5

NOT QUITE FORGOTTEN

TO: Monsieur Pierre Wagrez
    Superintendent Farm #4, Marconi River District, French Guyana
    Colony

FM: Directorate of Prison Affairs, Department of Justice

SUBJ: Citizen-Colonist Francois Barbe-Marbois

It is hereby directed that the subject Citizen-Colonist shall be, at the earliest convenience, returned to the Colonial Administration facility in Cayenne, where he shall await further transport to a penal facility on the Island of Oleron, Administration Department of Rochefort, France.

No further instruction.

Arnaud d'Estang By Direction

So, Francois. This is the end of our little collaboration here on the edge of civilization, eh. Back to France, even if it is a detention facility, on an island. You'll be able to see the lights of Rochefort at night, so close to *belle* France, you'll be able to smell her, almost taste her. I envy you, Francois." States Pierre.

"Maybe I am to be sent back to France for the guillotine? A public spectacle?" Speculates Francois.

"No, no, my friend. We have guillotines and spectators aplenty here in Guyana. If the Directorate wanted you dead, you'd be dead already. Rehabilitation, yes, it's rehabilitation for you, Francois. You are returned to Oleron, you sing their pretty song, *et voila*, you are free again. I think this is what is your future. You are much too intelligent, much too valuable to France to join those worthless, headless lordships and worships rotting in the ground. You have a future, Francois. Remember me, when you walk the halls of power again. Poor Pierre, who was kind, a brother to you here in the bogs of Guyana."

Ile d'Oleron is a long, narrow island in the south of the Bay of Biscay, on the western coast of France. Oleron shares the bay with Ile de Re to the north near La Rochelle, and the smaller Ile d'Aix fixed somewhat between its two larger neighbors. Between Oleron and Aix stands an "on again, off again" fortress battery of artillery, Fort Boyard. From northern Oleron, Aix or Ft. Boyard one can easily see mainland France and the city of Rochefort. Each of these islands, and fortress battery host French naval and coastal artillery forces, the strengths of which ebb and flow with events and the times. It is the partially forested, low-laying Oleron to which Francois is transported. There he is less engaged in useful industry, more subjected to political indoctrination and watched closely by his naval hosts. He is to be re-educated in the ways of the revolution, until the events of *18 Bumaire*, Year VIII of the revolution.

"Citizens, you long to be returned to France, to your families, I am certain. But first, here, in my care, you must be re-educated in the spirit of the revolution. Forget the Bourbon, the Bourbon is dead. Long live the French Republic. Long live *Liberte, Egalite et Fraternite.* Tell me Citizen Francois Barbe-Marbois, how does *Liberte, Egalitie et Fraternite* speak to your spirit?" Challenges *Premier-maitre* Charriere. Francois, seated on the compacted, sandy loam of the courtyard, rises to answer. "Citizen *Premier-maitre, Liberte* is freedom from despotic control. Be it the Bourbon, The Committee of Public Safety or the *Directoire, Liberte* be not present here. Only I am here, a stranger in my own land, separated from the ones I love."

"Citizen Marbois, it is such counter-revolutionary sentiments that bring you to this place.

You must accept the tenets of the revolution before you can enjoy its rewards. You are intelligent, but hard. Perhaps you may still learn."

Likened to birthing, France's revolution is spasmatic; 1) The Bastille is stormed on 14 July 1789, 2) absolute monarch Louis XVI and his family are moved from Versailles to The Tuileries palace in Paris where he can be more closely monitored by the revolutionaries, 3) Louis attempts to flee to his Austrian allies in 1792, 4) Louis and his Austrian-born queen Marie are arrested and returned to Paris, where they are charged with counter-revolution and treason, 5) Louis, desacralized, now known as Citizen Louis Capet, is guillotined along with his "foreign" queen in 1793, 6) The First Republic is declared, 7) The Reign of Terror, 8) Dechristianization of France, 9) France at war with England, Prussia, Austria-Hungary and Italian States suffers defeats, sees victories and 10) popular, young general, Napoleon Bonaparte, aided by his politician brother Lucien, overthrow the *Directoire* and establish The Consulate (Dictatorship) of France 1799.

Notes: 38) *Bumaire*, Fr., November of the French Revolutionary calendar, 39) Year VIII, Fr., 1799 on the French Revolutionary calendar, 40) *Premier-maitre*, Fr., Naval Chief Petty Officer

"Have you heard the latest news from Paris, Citizen Marbois?" Taunts *Premier-maitre* Charriere.

"Oh, yes, a seagull passing overhead shat the news on my head!" Replies Fracois peevishly.

"The Bonaparte brothers have overthrown *Le Directoire*, dissolved *Le Conseil des Cinq Cents* and established The Consulate. The dithering politicians scatter like roaches in the light. The revolutionary Constitution remains! *Vive La France*!

Within a month of the declaration of The Consulate, an important letter arrives from the mainland of France. The letter is addressed to Citizen Francois Barbe-Marbois, it bears the seal of the Ministry of Finance. A letter from Citizen Antoine Rene Charles Mathurin, Comte de Laforet.

November 15, 1799

Citizen Francois Barbe-Marbois,

I trust this letter finds you in good health and ready to rejoin the fraternity of citizens of the Republic of France. Your name has come to my attention, and at the urging of Citizen Minister Tallyrand, your case, that is, your denunciation and transportation were, perhaps harsh and unwarranted. As you know, these have been difficult times and many of us have suffered indignities or worse. Accordingly, you are released on your own recognizance effective immediately.

Citizen Marbois, your past service to the crown, and more recent election as an *Ancien* have been favorably noted. It is requested, that is, I urge to join me as my junior Finance Minister in the service of the Consulate and Republic of France. I am assured that your financial and diplomatic acumen can be used in the service of the Republic.

Should you decide to accept this offer, please join me here in Paris at your earliest convenience. Should you choose to decline, then you are at liberty to either remain in France as a private citizen or depart the country at will. This letter may be used as official evidence of your intentions, regardless of your decision.

Also, present this letter to Comandante at your camp, and he is hereby directed to provide you with 10 gold Louis d'Or for temporary subsistence.

Bon chance et viva la France!

Antoine Rene Charles Mathurin
Minister of Finance

CHAPTER 6

THE EMPEROR

January 1, 1800

My dearest Elizabeth, I am free again! Recently released from involuntary re-education at the garrison on the Ile of Oleron, I have made my way to Paris where I have taken a very humble apartment on the *Rive Droite*, Rue Montmartre. I should have you join me as soon as I can secure more satisfactory living arrangements and better understand how we shall fit in the government of this new regime, The Consulate.

I shall not make the same errors as when *Le Directoire* held the reins of power, neither shall I be silent, only I will not put to paper words which may be furtively read by those other than the intended reader. I sense that our new leader, this boy general and his brother, will not long be satisfied as *Consul* rather see himself as king. Perhaps I am wrong, only time will tell.

My immediate condition here consists of a small desk in the corner of the Ministry of Finance, but with salary, and the opportunity to observe and listen. My tasks have been simple, but I look forward to more substantive work soon.

Tell me of your family and yourself. Are you willing to return again to France and cast our lot with the Republic? No shame on you should you be unwilling. In that eventuality, I shall reassess my circumstances here and rejoin you in America.

Until I can feel your heartbeat within my palm and look into the shadows of your eyes, keep yourself only for me.

Your loving husband
Francois

Long before the revolutionary uprisings against King George III of England and Louis XVI of France, the English-speaking colonies of North America and that of New France engaged in a fierce struggle for ultimate control of the Northern hemisphere. This North American war or the French and Indian War as it is known, was, of course, merely a side-show to the greater conflict known as the Seven Years War in Europe. In this struggle, both sides made promises and representations to their indigenous allies and fought a proxy-like war in the territories which lasted almost nine years, not seven. In the end, the less populated regions of Quebec, the Ohio Valley, as well as the vibrant trading port of New Orleans were lost to France in a war of attrition to the better organized English colonies, the English army, Colonial militia and their Iroquois allies. Bourbon France ceded its North American territories not only to Britain but also to the dying kingdom and empire of Spain. The Treaty of Fontainebleau in 1763 sealed the fate of French interests in North America and transferred Orleans to Spanish colonial authority.

Under Spanish colonial rule New Orleans thrived. Free trade burgeoned between the port of New Orleans, Cuba and other Caribbean outposts on which Spain hung its fading empirical star.

Former French *habitants*, Spanish administrators, Spanish traders, slaves, mixed race people, a few Americans and a new class of free blacks mingled together in a polyglottic, multi-cultural pot that only those in the city and its environs could understand. Still, the vibrance, strength and strategic location of the city did no go unnoticed by the incoming administration of Thomas Jefferson, 3rd President of the new and expanding United States of America.

Spain, like France, struggled with uprisings, mismanagement and escalating expenses in the colonial administration of its territories in the New World. Resentment and rebellion simmered just below the façade of colonial governance. Early in this new century, the Viceroyalty of Peru would be the first, followed by Bolivia, Venezuela, Columbia and Mexico, to throw off the yoke of Spain rule. In 1800, after just 33 years of control, Spain retro-cedes New Orleans and the wild unknown of the Louisiana Territory back to France, Napoleon's France.

Bourbon, Directory or Consul, France finds itself involved in incessant wars on all frontiers.

The crowns of Europe loath and fear the radical ideas spawned by the French Republic. Putting aside centuries-old animosities and mistrust, entering into new alliances, the major powers of Europe face off with the French. In the Battle of the Nile, Horatio Lord Nelson deals the French a stinging maritime blow, proving English hegemony of the sea. The Hapsburgs of Austro-Hungary, mourning the death of their own, the late Queen Antoinette, look to put French heads on pikes. The Prussians and Bavarians take advantage of the chaos in Paris to adjust frontier boundaries and expand influence in the Low Countries. Spain too is drawn into the conflict over Sardinia and its common border. All of Europe is embroiled in conflict with French interests, save the Swiss and the Norse. Men are cheap, but guns and bullets are expensive.

The Consul seeks funds wherever funds can be found. The Consul turns to Citizen-Minister Mathurin.

"Let us, for the moment regard the globe here before us. Egypt is lost. We must cede the Near East to the English for the time being, until which, we can either decapitate the head of the English snake by crossing its Channel or by working with the Persians and attack the English underbelly in India. The Italian and Spanish fronts are stabilized. The Prussians and the Austrians remain a constant and immediate threat to the Republic. Hummm?"

The *Premier Consul,* Napoleon, points to the globe again as Foreign Minister Tallyrand and Finance Minister Mathurin look on.

Note: 41) *Le Premier Consul,* Fr., First Consul. Napoleon's title before crowning himself Emperor of France in 1804

"Here, in the Americas, we have drawn down our forces in Saint Dominigue, but remain strong in our other Caribbean territories. Perhaps we can leverage our newly reacquired territory of Louisiana with these land-hungry Americans, thereby replenishing our Treasury and ridding ourselves of expense at the same time? What do you think Mathurin? Tallyrand? Questions *Le Premier Consul.*

"I have a good man in Citizen Barbe-Marbois. He lived in America under *le ancien regime.* He is married to an American woman, or was before he was transported. He knows Jefferson, and others personally. Without question, he is the best man for the task." Responds Mathurin.

"Can he be trusted? He was denounced as a royalist." Comments Tallyrand.

"That is droll, Monsieur *le Bishop d'Autun.* If anyone should know better, it should be you!

In the Terror, everyone was suspect. Everyone was counter-revolutionary or royalist until proven otherwise, either before or after execution of sentence. We are all lucky to be here today! Yes, I believe he can be trusted as much as we trust ourselves. Does that answer your question, Monsieur?" Answers Mathurin without blinking an eye.

Napoleon intercedes. "Yes, that should suffice. Allow Citizen Marbois to develop a plan. I look forward to reading his proposal. Thank you"

Before Marbois' proposal is developed, another similar conversation is taking place on the other side of the Atlantic. A conversation within the new Jefferson Administration. In 1802, the United States Minister to France, Honorable Robert Livingston receives a letter from the President himself.

April 14, 1802

Hon. Robert Livingston Paris, France My dear Sir, I pray that this letter finds you in good health, and busy seeing to the important affairs of our nation in France. It has come to my attention, that Spain intends to return the port city of New Orleans and the unexplored region of Louisiana to the sovereignty of the Republic of France.

As you are well aware, our nation expands to the west. The port city of New Orleans and the Mississippi River valley and its tributaries are vital in the commerce of our western most states and to the expansion of our interests in the west. I believe that the United States should explore any opportunity to negotiate the purchase of the port city of New Orleans and those lands surrounding which the French may be willing to cede.

To this end, I have discussed this confidential matter with my good friend, Mr. James Monroe. I have asked him to consider joining you in Paris as Minister Extraordinary, in order to speedily explore and negotiate a deal with these French. As Mr. Monroe is a close ally, I expect his future assistance, post-negotiations, would be most valuable in the Congress.

Your understanding and candid thoughts on this matter and proposal would be most helpful as I hold your consul in highest regard.

Faithfully yours,
Thomas Jefferson

Even as James Monroe boards his ship for the long journey to Paris, Jefferson works with Secretary of State James Madison and Secretary of the Treasury Albert Gallatin in order to finalize both the details and goals of a proposed expedition. Over twenty years before, Jefferson discussed such an expedition to the unknown territories to the northwest with John Ledyard, an American explorer. He is further encouraged after reading of Alexander McKenzie's exploits across the barren plains of Canada, through the Rockies and to the Pacific only a year of two before. After less than two years in office as President, Jefferson, with Gallatin's help, petitions the Congress for $2,500 to fund a transcontinental expedition, seeking, among other things, a navigable river route to the Pacific. So resolute is his resolve, he never considers that the Livingston/Monroe negotiations in Paris could fail.

The Livingston/Monroe negotiating team are initially unaware of discussions in which *Le Premier Consul* and his ministers have already decided to curtail expansionism in the Americas in favor of a decisive effort in Europe. Nor are Livingston and Monroe aware that their own president is in contact with French nobleman Pierre Samuel du Pont de Nemours, thereby seeking the advantage of a two-prong strategy of information and negotiations.

France, seeking to deprive the English of the North American territories in the Treaty of Fontainebleu in 1783, now needs money to defeat the English on its homeland. General Le Clerc's disastrous expedition to Saint Dominigue, losing two-thirds of his force to tropical disease and the rebels only hastens the call and need for retrenchment. Marbois is aware of the strategic level decisions and the never-ending need for money. He can but only succeed in his negotiations with these Americans. The cat lives another life as his political star ascends once again.

In an unusual *menage a trois,* Livingston/Monroe, Marbois, and du Pont preform a ballet of negotiations on behalf of their puppet masters Napoleon and Jefferson. Money is difficult to come by in America, as mining exploration had been limited in America's colonial years, then what small production existed, ceased during the Revolutionary War. Only after the establishment of the U.S. Mint in 1792 did small coinage again become available; a steady but limited supply of copper coins primarily from Michigan copper ore, silver quarter, half and full dollar coin from the old Ethan Allen silver mine in Loudville, Massachusetts, and limited quarter, half and eagle gold coins from Reed's Mine in Cabarrus County, North Carolina. Due in part to Alexander Hamilton's valuation ratios, U.S. gold is undervalued on the world market, therefore what little exists, is in great demand. A sum of $15 million is agreed upon for the Louisiana Territory of which France really controls only New Orleans; friendly, curious, needy and hostile aborigines inhabit the interior. The eventual agreement and actual payment of $11.25 million in gold and $3.75 million in debt forgiveness for the Louisiana Territory, is of greater than face value to Napoleon in Europe as he prepares his country, army and self for another decade of war and strife.

Although Robert Livingston will stay as ambassador to Napoleon's France for another year or so, he pens a short letter to President Jefferson on the accomplishment.

Note: *Menage a trois,* Fr., threesome (generally used in a sexual context)

April 30, 1803

President Thomas Jefferson
The White House, Washington DC

Dear Mr. President,

It is with great pleasure that I inform you that an agreement has been reached and treaty signed this day, whereby France sells New Orleans and the Louisiana Territories to the United States of America for the total sum of $15 million; $11.25 in cash gold or silver coin or bullion, and $3.75 million in debt forgiveness. This represents a great victory for the future of the United States of America.

"We have lived long but this is the noblest work of our whole lives... The United States take rank this day among the first powers of the world."

Mr. Monroe has been of great assistance in this matter and deserves recognition for such, as does the esteemed Monsieur du Pont.

I will continue my work here in France at your pleasure, sir, or as long as the Lord may grant me strength of mind and body.

Your most humble servant
Robert Livingston

CHAPTER 7

PREPARATIONS

Meriwether, in your position here as my Secretary, and with your knowledge of the officers, their politics and standing as well as those of the ranks, I think it should be you to form a unit, a Corps of Discovery, to explore the northwestern territories." Explains Jefferson.

"Mr. President? I am certain that there are others who better qualify for such a herculean task." Replies Lewis.

"Yes, there are always others. But with you; a fellow Virginian of Albemarle County, a confidant and friend, an Army man, one of strong organization skills and leadership. Yes, there may be others, but it is you whom I can trust to execute my will in this great adventure as no other man I know." Exclaims Jefferson "Even the Roman Emperor Caligula was only known as "little boots", with this charge, you have asked me to fill some very large boots indeed!" Quips Meriwether.

"Who will be your second in command, Meriwether?" Asks Jefferson casually.

"Second Lieutenant William Clark. The Army has denied him a captaincy, sir."

"Do I know him?"

"No, I think not, sir. I actually served under him in the Virginia Militia."

"Do you think it wise to bring on a former superior officer as your subordinate here?" Asks Jefferson somewhat concerned.

"No, Mr. President, I do not see this as a problem. Clark is also Virginia born. He was raised however, in the western wilderness of Kentucky, and is familiar with privation and practices of the aborigines. He is organized, and conscientious. Regardless of our formal ranks, I will address him as Captain, for the sake of the men. He will command as my equal, only be directed to duties such as cartography, supply and Indian relations. This mission is bigger than one man, sir. I need a strong and capable second."

"Very well, Meriwether. I will outline my expectations; you decide with whom and how to succeed in this monumental task. You have my fullest confidence."

Meriwether begins preparations, first by hand-picking the unit. He draws primarily from those he knows, either in person or by reputation, from the Army. William Clark assists him in this matter, but is already more engaged in supply. Among the unit's other members, 5 are non-commissioned officers, and 30 are enlisted ranks. The only regular Army sergeant is Sergeant John Ordway, Yankee born, from the U.S. First Infantry Regiment. There is a French-Canadian hunter/interpreter, Monsieur George Douillard, who later with Sacagawea, the teenaged wife of another French-Canadian member, Toussaint Charbonneau, are to become among the most valued members of the expedition. Monsieur Charbonneau however, is described as "a man of no particular merit." Without the hunter and interpretive skills of Douillard and the geographic knowledge and soft skills of the young native American mother, the expedition would have been crippled from the start. Lt. Clark's inherited, enslaved companion York joins the party as does Seaman, Meriwether's Newfoundland dog. There are contract civilians, mostly of French descent, keelboatmen who will accompany the expedition only as far as the winter encampment. These men and their keelboat will carry men and supplies to what will become "Fort" Mandan, then return the next spring with reports, journals, maps and flora/fauna samples, including a live prairie dog, for speedy delivery to any anxious President.

The officers and men, as well as the civilian guides and boatmen have heard tall tales of the western wilderness. In the western expanses roam hostile aborigines, giant man-eating bears, and barren landscapes without water and without end. Yet, also known is that Mountain Men, many former French *habitants,* some Americans either seeking or running have wandered into the western unknown and lived to tell their tales. So, it is generally understood that given the proper equipment, training and preparations, the largely unknown lands west of the Mississippi are survivable. With these thoughts in mind, Capt. Lewis establishes a training camp along the Wood River at its confluence to the mighty Mississippi, safely on the east bank in American territory. Here Lewis & Clark will begin to prepare and train the regular men for the long adventure to come, across the great Mississippi then up the mighty Missouri River, as far as it will take them, some hundreds, perhaps thousands of miles. The contract men will arrive later.

CHAPTER 8

THE MEN

Born into the ruling, land-owning gentry of Old Dominion, Meriwether Lewis, experiences life and tragedies typical of American colonials of the day; no early formal education, a father dying when he is young, relocation by a step-father, in this case, to Cherokee country in Georgia and much time to himself watching, listening and learning the skills of a hunter and outdoorsman. Meriwether develops much empathy for the native Cherokee people in Georgia upon whose land the white settlers now encroach and many of whom, later, under populist Andrew Jackson will be exiled to Indian Territory, forced onto the Trail of Tears.

Later, as luck would have it, he is sent back to his native Virginia under the guardianship of his natural uncle Nicolas Lewis and formally educated by private tutors, later at Liberty Hall Academy, a liberal arts institution founded by non-sectarian Scot-Irish.

Upon graduation Meriwether joins the Virginia Militia and participates in an action known as the Whiskey Insurrection, one of the earliest tax protests in the United States of America.

About the same time, he is initiated into the Society of Freemasons, a secretive, and popular institution in the day. Typical of the "ruling" class of Old Dominion, Meriwether is interested in politics, noticed and promoted by another Virginian and founding father, Thomas Jefferson.

Soon after his inauguration as the third President, Meriwether is called upon to become Secretary to the President in April 1801.

"An imposing wall stands before this country, and its exploration and interests in the West, Meriwether. That wall is the great river, The Mississippi. Though a wall, this river and its tributaries are also conduits into that mysterious land. The key and gateway to that which is beyond the Mississippi is New Orleans. We must possess that city if we are to tap all the greatness which the West entices. To this end, Messieurs Livingston and Monroe are to negotiate with the French. I also have another, shall we say, "backdoor" channel, which I may use as a source of "inside" information." Explains the President.

"Very wise, sir. I look forward to the eventuality of our successful negotiations with General Napoleon. I know that economics drives your efforts, but, I suspect also your deep, life-long interest in the natural sciences. I confess that I have similar interests, surely not as passionate as your own, but another more secret hobby, that of Paleontology. I have always been fascinated by the deep past, those histories not readily apparent to modern societies. As a younger man, I spent much time among the indigenous peoples of the southeast, mostly the Cherokee. I listened to their stories of the lands beyond the great river; tales of bones, the great man-devouring bears, the so-called hairy ones, large men-like beings who had no tribe, and animals described as pachyderms with huge curving tusks, legs like giant tree stumps and coats of thick, dangling buffalo mane. My passion is to investigate these stories and discern fact from fiction. Who knows, perhaps I will make a discovery which will change our view of the past." Expounds Meriwether.

"An exciting passion indeed, Meriwether. It is hard to imagine ape men or furry elephants wandering about the West but even the wildest tale often has some semblance of fact in its foundation. We shall seek out these facts together. Continues the President. Now,

Meriwether, tell me some about your second, Lieutenant William Clark."

"I have known him or known of him for more than a decade, sir. He hails from a large family from King and Queen County. He is several years older than myself. Although a native Virginian, like ourselves, he, like myself, was transplanted outside of Virginia as a young man and grew-up near Louisville in Kentucky. He has spent much time in the wilderness thereabouts and is a skilled man in the woods. He understands the natives and has accepted some of their customs as his own. Unlike myself he has travelled the Ohio on a flatboat but as myself has military experience and has fought the Indian. He has experience as an Adjutant and Quartermaster. I need his experience in force organization and supply. Without the utmost organization and supply planning, our expedition to the Northwest will fail in a short time. He will do us good. My only concern is the state of his health. He resigned from the militia a few years ago due to poor health. What constituted that "poor" health, I do not know. But he currently manages the family plantation of Mulberry Hill, no easy task to be sure. I will correspond with him, inquiring therein about his health. I am confident that he will join us with enthusiasm, Mr. President." Outlines Meriwether.

"Very well. I have a fine Madeira here, Meriwether. Will you join me in a toast to the success of "our" expedition?" Proposes the President.

Fine crystal rings upon its equal, as Captain Meriwether Lewis and President Thomas Jefferson toast the proposed expedition.

May 2, 1801

Captain William Clark
Mulberry Hill Plantation, Kentucky

Dear Captain Clark,

I pray that this letter finds you in good health and prosperity. You may remember me as Ensign Meriwether Lewis. I served with you in the Militia under General Charles Scott. I trust that your recollection of myself and service as being favorable.

Presently I serve at the pleasure of the President. He has charged me in organizing an expedition to the Northwest. There are certain negotiations taking place between our country, the French and Spanish in regards to the future of this territory. It is the position of the Jefferson Administration to acquire, minimally, the port city of New Orleans and some lands in that vicinity. Regardless, the vast lands to the northwest, across the great mountains and to the Pacific are void of civilization, the home of beasts and a few nomadic tribes. It is this territory that I have been tasked with; the survey of both land and navigable water routes, the cataloguing flora & fauna and the indexing and peaceful negotiations with the various aboriginal tribes.

I recall your presence of command, organizational and quartermaster abilities. I believe your participation in this venture would be most valuable and have expressed such to the President.

To this end, I propose that you join me as my Lieutenant and equal in command. Your Lieutenancy is only a matter of formality with War Department, you no doubt recall how the Army can be concerning issues of seniority. I will address you as Captain and we shall command jointly. We can expect to be in the field two to three years. This is an opportunity of a lifetime.

Thank you in advance for your serious consideration of this proposal. Should you be favorably inclined, please write me as soon as possible for additional details.

Most sincerely, Meriwether Lewis,
Secretary to the President.

June 7, 1801

Secretary Meriwether Lewis
White House, Washington D.C.

Dear Secretary Lewis,

I am in receipt of your letter dated May 2, and am humbled by the offer contained therein. That you and the President should consider my participation in the expedition as "most valuable", how could I but accept the invitation of my President?

You inquired as to my health. I am happy to report that I have seemingly fully recovered from such disorders of the stomach and bowels which also troubled me greatly for a time along with great fatigue. Home and hearth of Mulberry Hill Plantation have no doubt contributed to my rapid recovery and I see no impediment to my full participation in the expedition.

I have previously made the acquaintance of a Sergeant John Ordway, a tough New Hampshire man who was, at the time of my serving, in the Army and who would be my choice as a senior Non-Commissioned Officer if that billet were still available. He is an educated man, familiar with both the wilderness, and aboriginal customs. He is an outstanding organizer and leader of men. He would be an exceptional additional to the company.

I am not overly concerned about the specifics of the expedition at this time. Know ye that I will make myself available at the time and place of your choosing. Further, please feel free to task me with any specific pre-planning requirements you may deem within my experiences.

Thank you and the President again for considering me for this great adventure.

Most respectfully,
William Clark

"Good Morning, Mr. President. I am pleased to inform you that I have received a letter from Captain Clark in which he has agreed to join your Corps of Discovery. He further recommends a regular Army sergeant by the name of John Ordway. I am unfamiliar with the man, but Capt. Clark speaks highly of him. I will inquire of the man and check his records. Should I be satisfied, then, with your permission, I will ask him to join the Corps along with, his choice, of nine men, from amongst those at his post. Volunteers everyone, of course." Says Meriwether.

"A capital idea. Our little "mustard seed" begins to grow. Glows the President. Sooner than you think, you may be confronting one of those hairy ape-like men of yours or chasing down the wooly pachyderm. I, on the other hand, foresee steamboats churning their way along a Northwest Passage all the way to the Pacific. Can you even imagine what that would do for commerce and development? I have never forgotten Fitch's steamboat demonstrating on the Delaware in the presence of we members of the Constitutional Convention. No steamboat has yet seen the Mississippi, but it won't be long." Muses the President.

"Sir. Ape-men, beasts of all shapes and sizes, an inviting waterway, a gateway to China, our manifest fantasies. But first we must fund, recruit, organize, and supply this little adventure of ours." Reminds Meriwether.

"Oh yes, I know. You rob me of my moment of musings. I am planning to petition the Congress for $2,500 to fund the Corps." States Jefferson.

"$2,500? That is hardly enough, I think, Mr. President." Retorts Meriwether.

"Yes, I agree. But a proper outfitting may very well bring about additional scrutiny from those holding our purse strings. A miserly amount may not draw their attention. You'll have to live off the land sooner than later and make trade with the tribes. To this end, I am planning some shiny, silver Peace Medals be struck, and of course the usual trade goods. Have you thought much about a guide and interpreters?" Asks Jefferson

"For the past hundred years or more the French have been plying the waters of the Ohio, and Mississippi watersheds. St. Louis has always been a gateway and center of these activities.

It is in St Louis where I intend to make inquiries when the expedition's organization and timetables are finalized. I expect to have few problems in engaging the right man or men for the job. After all, St Louis is also known as *Pain Court*, translated "short of bread" for its lack of jobs and food. A brace of opportunity hungry Frenchmen should not prove problematic" Replies Meriwether confidently.

"Good. Work with your man Clark and make your preparations. I will provide a list of my priorities and a "start" date. I expect to be in the spring or summer of '03. States Jefferson.

"When the time comes, I plan to make our depot and "jump-off" point just north of *Pain Court*. We shall ascend the waters of the Pekitanoui as *Pere* Marquette would have said and begin our investigations with the Oumessourita, the Missouri tribe located there. I will keep you duly informed, Mr. President." Finishes Meriwether.

Meriwether keeps his pledge to the President as he serves double duty as Secretary and Commander of the nascent Corps of Discovery. By mid-spring 1803 formalities are complete, documents are exchanged and Lewis prepares to move his "flag" to Camp Dubois, just north of St. Louis and short canoe ride across the Mississippi to this Missouri River and the beginning.

Chapter 8

CAMP DU BOIS

For one to say that Camp Du Bois was hewn out of the western wilderness, is simply not true. Camp Du Bois was occupied. The Captain, Meriwether Lewis, chose to occupy one of the many existing "syruper" camps along the eastern shores of the Mississippi Valley and its valleys of tributaries. Maple or other syrups being cheaper and more readily available to folks in the western territories than cane sugar or molasses grown, processed and shipped from the Caribbean, these seasonal camps proliferated in the area north of St Louis.

After having bade farewell and departed the White House, the former Secretary, now Captain Meriwether Lewis is transported up the Potomac River, past its five great falls, along The Potomac Company's skirting canals to Cumberland, Maryland where the navigable river meets the old Braddock Road across the Alleghenies. The so-called Braddock Road is named after British General Edward Braddock, who in 1755 led two regiments of British regulars and some Colonial militia along this route toward Fort Duquesne during the French and Indian Wars. Braddock disastrously underestimated the tenacity of the French and their Indian allies, and paid dearly for it with his life. Still, the trace, now rough road, bears his name for eternity.

Overland from Cumberland to Pittsburg, the old Fort Duquesne, Lewis rides or leads a horse. In Pittsburg he is waylaid for a period of time awaiting the completion of his keelboat. It is in Pittsburg that another, to be valued, member of the Corps joins, Seaman, a black Newfoundland dog which Lewis purchases for $20.

Lewis hires civilian keelboatmen for the trip first to Louisville, Kentucky, St. Louis, Camp Du Bois and ultimately the long expedition ahead. Some will stay on, others won't, but, in any case, Lewis and Seaman board their new keelboat and begin the next leg of the journey to Louisville, Kentucky, a riverport near Mulberry Hill Plantation where Lieutenant William Clark anxiously await his new commander.

By correspondence Lewis expects Lieutenant Clark to meet him in Louisville, a growing riverport town named so in honor of Louis of France. Some 25 years before, Col. George Rogers Clark of the Continental Army had secretly established a communication outpost on Corn Island under the guise of assisting 80 settlers from Pennsylvania. This was the beginning of Louisville.

The 600 odd mile journey from Pittsburgh, Pennsylvania to Louisville, the new state of Kentucky, passes quickly. The boat is new, the civilian keelboat men experienced and the current swift enough. After three weeks, the boat ties up to a makeshift pier at Louisville on the south bank of the river.

A big Negro man sits on the pier, waiting.

"You be Captem Lewis?" Asks the big man.

"Yes, I am Captain Lewis. And who may you be?" Replies Lewis.

"I be York, Captem. I be sent here by Masta Clark. Answers York. Masta Clark expects you must be tired and needing a good place to rest. I will show you to Louisville's best hotel. It was built about ten year ago. Then I go fetch my Masta."

"Thank you, York. Allow me to gather my sack from the boat and make arrangements for Seaman, my dog. I will be with you shortly." Explains Lewis.

"Masta Clark be coming as soon as I can get back home and tell em that you is here. He say that I be coming with you too!" Informs York.

"Is that a fact? I hadn't considered the inclusion of personal servants in the group. I shall have to discuss this matter in more detail with Lieutenant Clark. Do you want to go, York?" Asks Lewis.

"I do what the Masta says, Captem." replies York without looking at Lewis The next morning Lieutenant William Clark reports to his commander, Captain Meriwether Lewis, for duty. His personal baggage is small and well packed in oilskins. York accompanies his master as Seaman accompanies Lewis.

"Lieutenant William Clark reporting for duty, sir. And welcome to Kentucky." States Clark somewhat less than formally.

"Good Morning "Captain" Clark. Good to see you again. I did not set this early hour as the time of our meeting. I trust that such an early rising has not inconvenienced you?"

"No, sir. Not at all. I am accustomed to rising early with the plantation. The most productive work is accomplished in the morning. We must take advantage of the hour." Explains Clark.

"Yes, with the plantation. I understand. That does bring us to a question I have. I did not expect you to join in the company of a servant. I am not certain how I feel about this? True, he is a big man, broad across the back, but his presence may cause some disharmony amongst the men." States Lewis.

"Of course, it is your prerogative to decline him, but he is my man, since childhood, not a fieldhand. Truthfully, he has caused me some trouble of late and I have contemplated hiring him out to someone more stern than myself (See Note 42). I thought that another strong back and the western air might be good for both the mission and York. Your prerogative, sir?"

Note: 42) Correspondence between William Clark and his older brother Jonathan Clark support these assertions re: York.

"You and I, Clark, are of the same blood. Although our families immigrated here, we are both Irish or Scot or Scot-Irish, born, bred, and hailing from the Old Dominion – Virginia. We are Caucasian by race, European by origin, Americans by choice. This man of yours, York. He has had no choices in his life. He is "your" man, your property, given to you when you were a young man. Who knows what his tribe was or where his father, or his father's father hails from? We know only that he is not like us. Racially he is a Negro. His people come, not by choice, from the continent of Africa. He may be American by geography, but he does not enjoy the same rights as us. I think that the time has come for York to make his own choices. It IS my prerogative, so I say that if he comes on this expedition, at least for the duration of the expedition, York is a free man. He will share the same comforts and trials, he will be allowed to make his voice be heard. He will no longer be your man, but a full-fledged member of the Corps of Discovery. These are my terms, Clark. If you agree, we will ask him whether or not he wishes to join the expedition as a volunteer. If you do not agree, then it is my decision that you send him home now." States Lewis flatly and without emotion. "It is now your prerogative to choose, sir?"

A bit taken back by Meriwether Lewis' unexpectedly liberal interpretation of the Rights of Man, not so subtle admonishment of the South's "peculiar institution" and distaste for Clark's own slave owning, Clark stands awkwardly for a moment, absent of reply. He recovers his composure quickly however, looks Lewis directly in the eye, then turns and addresses York.

"York, choose! You may come along, a free and equal member of the expedition or you may go home to your wife. Your choice, not mine."

York hesitates for a moment then says. "I chooses to go with you, Masta Clark."

"Very good, York. But remember, this is a military expedition. If you run away and are caught, you will not be sent home, admonished and whipped, you will be shot." States Clark coldly. "And I am not longer then

The Master. Your will address me as Lieutenant, Sir. Do you understand, York?" Furthers instructs Clark.

"Yes, Masta, I, I means Lieutenant, Sir."

"It is settled then. Concludes Lewis. And you, Lieutenant William Clark, you and I will have a goodly two to three years to sophisize the Rights of Man."

"A formidable gantlet you throw down, sir. I accept the challenge." Smiles Clark.

After this short exchange, the three men walk down muddy Center Street toward the river and the makeshift pier where the keelboat is tied up. Boarding the boat, they are greeted by Seaman. Their meagre luggage is stowed below, the order is given and the keelboat is poled away from shore, into the current of the mighty Ohio, toward Corn Island and beyond.

From Louisville it is less than 400 miles to its confluence with the Mississippi. It is not a deep river, averaging only 15 feet in depth, with a current of only one to two miles per hour. But the Ohi-yo (Seneca language), meaning "good river" can be treacherous and unforgiving, its muddy waters hiding damaging debris, shoals and hazards.

For the most part, the keelboatmen are experienced and hard working. The Mississippi River is reached in the relatively short time of just two weeks. Now the more difficult task begins, a prelude to the arduous days ahead; poling, rowing, sometimes sailing against the current of Mississippi to St Louis and just beyond, Camp Du Bois. The Missouri River however will sorely test the mettle of the men, its waters rush south by southeast at three to five miles per hour, a harsh reality that the expedition will have to endure for it's 2,341 mile length. Swift current, harsh weather, hostile tribes and beasts yet unknown all await the little Corps of men just beyond the horizon and the warm campfires of Camp Du Bois.

The riverport "Gateway To The West, St. Louis, is disappointing. The ramshackle collection of buildings, muddy streets, unattractive citizens and visitors alike, make a less than positive impression on the already gloomy

Captain Lewis. Meriwether directs Clark to gather some additional, basic supplies in St. Louis, where he can obtain these on U.S. government vouchers while preserving his small cache of hard specie for the remainder of the journey. Whether or not he will, in fact, even be able to use coin beyond St. Louis remains a question, but the chances of using coin west of the Mississippi are nevertheless greater than the chances of using U.S. Promissory Vouchers.

The officers' manpower and supply business is concluded by late mid-day and it is decided to continue up river toward Camp Du Bois, where Sergeant Ordway and a short platoon of 30+ regular U.S. Army volunteers are already assembled.

Sergeant Ordway has already turned the "syruper's squat" into a more organized military encampment. Shelters are orderly, water, wood and latrines have been prepared. The men are organized into details including; guard, wood-cutting, foraging and mess. Lewis is not disappointed with the preparations made by this Sergeant previously unknown to him.

The assembled volunteers are, of the most part, regular U.S. Army men, privates from both the 1st and 2nd U.S. Infantry Regiments. Meriwether observes and familiarizes himself with the men and their interactions over the next few days. Given those observations and the recommendations of both Lieutenant Clark and Sergeant Ordway, 3 men are promoted to sergeant and 1 promoted to corporal. This brings the complement to; 30 privates, 5 non-commissioned officers including 4 sergeants and 1 corporal, Monsieur Drouillard, the guide, hunter and interpreter, a dozen or so French *habitants* keelboatmen and, of course, York, Clark's soon to be emancipated man servant and Seaman, boat dog extraordinaire.

"Captain Clark, please inform the company that we shall break camp at dawn, board our vessels and enter the Missouri on the morrow. My compliments, sir." Orders Captain Lewis.

A full two years have now passed since Thomas Jefferson proposed that he, Meriwether Lewis should form and command The Corps of Discovery.

Concurrent to Lewis' preparations, negotiations were successfully entered into and concluded with both the Spanish and the French as New Orleans is first retro-ceded back to the French, then resold to the Americans, along with untold millions of square miles of under-explored territory to become know collectively as the Louisiana Purchase.

Secretary, that is, now Captain Meriwether Lewis departed his comfortable position at the White House in the mid-summer of 1803. His somewhat circuitous journey to Camp Du Bois took him up the Potomac to Cumberland, along the old Braddock Trace to Pittsburg, down the Ohio River to Louisville, Kentucky, to the Ohio's confluence with the Mississippi, to St. Louis and finally to the syruper's squat, Camp Du Bois. It is December 1803. Lewis, Clark and the Corps await the formal transfer of the territory from France to the United States of America. As they wait, they prepare; they drill and they winter, there on the Wood River on the edge of civilization.

Chapter 9

BIRD WOMAN

The Shoshone are a proud people inhabiting the mostly western slopes of the Great Mountains. Years before some tribal clans moved north toward the land of the Crow, while others moved east, encroaching the land of the Lakota. Consequently, both the Crow and the Lakota would become century long enemies of the Shoshone as they all compete for resources, poach remudas, raid and steal each other's women and children. Somewhat less warlike then their Lakota and Crow brethren, encounters, skirmishes and battles most often end with a Shoshoni defeat in spite of their utmost efforts.

Sacagawea was only 12 years old when she was torn from her family and village in a vicious Lakota counter-attack precipitated by the theft of a few under-fed, overworked ponies. A pitiful trade for the Shoshoni.

Young Sacagawea grabbed in the melee, her mother bludgeoned but not killed, her siblings scattered. She, healthy, and near puberty is a great prize, yet she is treated roughly. Her wrists are bound with rawhide lashings and she is flung onto a horse behind her captor. They ride swiftly toward the east into a sea of buffalo grass. The horse is lathered and breathes hard but does not stop. Her kidnapper neither looks nor speaks to her. What good would it do for him to speak? She does not speak Lakota. She speaks her native dialect, the ancient Ute-Aztec tongue of her people. She urinates astraddle the horse as it runs. She is offered no rest, no water. How has she offended the Spirits so?

Life with an enemy is never quite what one imagines. True, the Lakota, like the Shoshone, are a mobile and nomadic people. However, whereas the Lakota culture is Buffalo or *Tatanka*-centric, the Shoshone are somewhat less reliant on the Buffalo, more diversified in their staples and culture. Sacagawea is Shoshoni of the Lemhi Band, the more northernly band of the Shoshone. Usually, it would be the Crow with whom they compete, but unfortunately, it was a Lakota remuda which was raided and now Sacagawea finds herself being taken east, far from the Great Mountains, and deep into Lakota lands. She already knows in her heart that she will most likely never see her people again.

After what seems to be a day and a night, the kidnapper's pace begins to slacken. It is now unlikely that any Shoshoni would pursue them this far into Lakota territory. She is allowed to dismount, drink from a small stream and is given a piece of dried Buffalo to eat. Her tether however, is not removed nor is it loosened. Her hands are red and swollen from the tightness of the tether which is then fastened to a stake in the ground. Even a dog would not be so ill-treated in her village.

Life is hard among the Lakota. No respite, no kindness is shown to the young Shoshone captive. She must work to eat, work that tires even a young and healthy body. The men talk. The men smoke. The men hunt and sometimes draw blood from their indigenous brethren, but counting coup brings a Lakota warrior even higher praise from amongst his peers. To simply strike the enemy with a coup stick or the blunt end of a lance, exposing one's self to great danger, this act brings the highest praise.

The women garner no praise. The women butcher the kill, cure the hides, prepare the meals, stich clothing, bear and rear the next generations and maintain the daily life of the village. The women are married young and yet are left to die alone when they are no longer useful.

Still, in her heart, by virtue of her youth, Sacagawea clings to the smallest sliver of hope.

Just what she hopes for, she is not certain, but hope remains in her heart, hidden there in the deepest recesses of her being. "May the Creator of my soul, may the Great Spirit give my life purpose and have mercy on my being."

For more than two years the young girl, known as Bird Woman or Sacagawea serves her Hidatsa Lakota masters. She serves not only her kidnapper but every man, woman and even child in the village. Although she has experienced her first moon and her breasts have begun to develop beneath her elk-hide dress, the Great Spirit, in its omnipotence, has protected her from the wanton passions of the young men in the village. Fortunately, the young men concern themselves with their Coming-of-Age ceremony and the hunter-warrior skills that are required of it. They are too busy and too tired to exert any extra effort on a girl, a girl who can not even properly speak their tongue, a girl who looks, even smells different. From an early age, these young men have been taught to be Hidatsa-centric, and at least for now, they have retained those lessons.

Not of the Hidatsa however is an itinerant, white trapper, a *habitant* name Toussaint Charbonneau from far off Quebec, land of the Anishinaabeg or Algonquin nation. For a time, Charbonneau was permitted to live among the Hidatsa. The white man learned the Hidatsa tongue and often brought goods from a place he called *Rendezvous* to the southwest. Monsieur Tou loved to tempt the village men with these hard to acquire goods, but refrained from simply trading or selling them. To the men's delight, Monsieur Tou preferred to gamble. A loss of a few pelts is nothing when compared to gaining a bright, red, woolen blanket, an iron pot, a spoon, a shiny knife or even a rifle. Monsieur Tou was not interested in the Hidatsa's most precious possessions, their ponies, but he did have a powerful passion for the squaws. He loved to play with the squaws, young, mature or in-between. This could, of course, been a problem had the Hidatsa, in general, not thought so little of them.

One night while gaming with Sacagawea's captor, Monsieur Tou offers an iron pot, then a spoon and adds a large, shiny hunting knife to the lot in exchange for a chance at the Shoshoni girl. It is agreed. In a burst of fortune, Monsieur Tou wins Bird Woman with a toss of the dice.

To lose a useful slave is disappointing to her captor, but one less mouth to fed is also a relief to him. Sacagawea is now Toussaint Charbonneau's problem, if consummated, his wife.

Toussaint lingers with the Hidatsa only a day or two longer in order that the men may have a chance to win something from him, thus maintaining the equilibrium in their fragile relationship. He eventually loses the goods he had brought to trade; the bright, red, woolen blanket, the iron pot, the silver spoon, the shiny knife, even a rifle, not, of course, his .54 cal. Hawkins gun but a cheaper trade model. He departs the village however with yet another young woman, so much the better for his domestic needs, his passions and more warmth in the night.

Toussaint and company bid farewell to their wild hosts and move east, overland. He has become a baggage train of women, pelts, and supplies. He hopes to settle in with the Mandan for a spell, taking advantage of their less volatile, hospitable character and substantial, warm, mud-waddle lodges for the winter. He speaks better Mandan than Lakota and may even offload his pelts, if an upriver trader is willing to offer him a fair price. He considers his prospects as the little group make their way across the vast grasslands toward the morning sun.

Notes: 43) Hidatsa are a sub-group of the Lakota, 44) Trapper's *Rendezvous* organized by William Henry Ashley, Henry's Rocky Mountain Fur Company in 1825 and last until 1840. This was originally a gathering of Henry's Hundred. Earlier, less organized events no doubt took place.

Chapter 10

IT BEGINS

For lack of a bugle or drum, Sergeant Ordway uses his own motherly methods to coax the men from their slumber. It is an unnatural time to stir. It is still and dark the men are sleeping, snoring, dreaming hard, the dawn has not yet broke the eastern horizon. Most men stir at the sound of Sergeant Ordway's raspy voice, others are unlucky enough to feel the impact of his boot on some body part. In spite of the dark, within minutes of his pleasure, the company is awake, up, moving and preparing either their person, their breakfast and in the act of breaking camp. Preparations complete, the company is packed and assembled for departure as the sun breaks the horizon spreading its light across the fog-shrouded waters of the Mississippi.

The keelboat and pirogues are rowed and paddled across the great river toward the confluence of the Missouri's, rapid, stirring waters. Clark assumes operational command as Lewis sits and broods. For two years the expedition has been a dream to be discussed, planned and prepared for. The actual execution of the plan brings him no joy, almost an after the fact depression, a dissatisfaction with reality. Within hours however, Lewis' depression begins to dissipate along with the fog of the Mississippi. Entering the wild waters of the Missouri stir emotional excitement within him, and an adrenal charge to his body. He is Captain Meriwether Lewis again.

The cadence of the rowing, the rapidity of the paddling increases as the vessels fight the eddies and current of the oncoming river. The men are not used to the unending rhythm and routine of pushing, rowing, and paddling hour upon hour. By day's end they are played out and exhausted. A good, but inauspicious beginning Lewis thinks. We will break here for a rest and lunch. The order is given and the vessels turn toward the eastern shore of the Missouri where they are pulled up and staked. Lunch will be prepared ashore.

Lewis recognizes that his "green" Corps is nearly done in by the morning's exertions. He orders a two hour break during which the men have time to make fires, and prepare Johnny cakes, bacon and coffee. It is still too early in the expedition to forage for subsistence, so a little cornmeal, boiling water and salt make for a hearty and familiar meal, as well as coffee and bacon. Both of the latter two stables will be all too soon exhausted and native replacements will have to do. With any luck, the Corp's supply of cornmeal will last several months. Lewis plans to work upstream the Missouri for another three hours, this first day. A strong camp will be made late in the afternoon to allow for wood gathering, a bit of hunting and reconnaissance by Monsieur Drouillard and of course meal preparation, as well as a plug of tobacco, and a dram of whiskey to soften the effects of the day. Private Pierre Cruzatte takes up his fiddle and plays a tune whilst the men eat their evening ration. With the exception of tired muscles and the guard, not much seems different from camp life at Camp Du Bois. A squad of men are posted as sentries, relieved every four hours for their first night in this new and unknown land.

Sleeping while on guard duty is known to be a capital offense. But the guard wouldn't think of sleeping in this land of unknown beasts, Ape men and hostile Indians. Monsieur Drouillard bags no game on this first day, but a few fine fish are pulled from the muddy waters of the Missouri.

Many more fish will be needed to feed and satisfy the hungry men of this Corps of Discovery.

Reveille on the morning of the second day, like the first day, is the sound of Sergeant Ordway's gruff voice and the soft thud of his boot colliding with the ribs of an unlucky private not quick enough to suit him.

On the recommendation of Lieutenant Clark, Charles Floyd was promoted to sergeant before the company had departed Camp Du Bois. Sergeant Floyd was a literate man, hailing from the same Virginia stock as his commanders and a shirt-tail relation to both Lieutenant Clark and Virginia Governor John Floyd. Lewis has noted that Sergeant Floyd takes time each day to write in an unofficial journal. He wonders just what his newly minted sergeant is writing, but has yet to query him on the matter. On the first evening, after completing his assigned duties, Sergeant Floyd sits at his bivouac and pens a short note.

My Journal, Charles Floyd

May 14, 1804 – Today we advanced up the Missouri bout six miles. The weather is fair, but the waters of the Missouri are muddy and current is swift, much different than the currents of the Mississippi and Ohio. We all joined this expedition as volunteers. The success or failure is carried on the shoulders of each of us. These shoulders are already sore. We have a goodly task ahead. Sergeant Patrick Gass caught some fish, pike, I think.

The second day begins unlike the first, but similar to the next to the next eight months ahead of the little Corps. The men break camp, trying always to remain one step ahead of Sergeant Ordway's roaring voice and heavy boot. Brouillard, with his new Hawkins .54 caliber Plains rifle, walks along the eastern bank of the river in search of sign and game, two-legged or four. He does not regret not being part of the poling, rowing and paddling company struggling again the muddy spring current of the river. He has chosen to carry his Hawkins over the new Austrian .46 caliber, Girardoni air rifles brought along on the expedition. While novel, with their 20 shot magazine, recoilless, quiet and smokeless discharge, new-fangled gadgets do not move him with excitement. Drouillard prefers the age old and the proven although the flintlock is a marked improvement over the old matchlock rifle of his granddaddy. Feeding 50 hungry men each day is no easy task, but a task which he is more suited that poling. Today, Drouillard flushes only small game; rabbits, quail and a few prairie chickens. The quail are not worth his time, but rabbit stew would satisfy the men as would a spit-roasted prairie chicken. It is more cumbersome to carry two guns, but he will sling the Hawkins after lunch and carry a scattergun this afternoon.

During the lunch hour Lewis pens some notes to be reviewed latter in the day.

Temperature 77 degrees, bright and clear. Light wind from the southwest, barometer steady, no inclement weather forecast. Another good day or two ahead.

The first report of Drouillard's scattergun unsettles the men. They furtively scan the river bank for sign of an aboriginal hunting party proudly carrying the Drouillard's freshly parted scalp. The second report of the gun, gives them pause to analyze the first. The dull thud of a scattergun, quite unlike the sharp report of a rifle. Drouillard must be after small game.

Anxiety turns to anticipation as the men fantasize of rabbit stew or roast bird for their supper.

Although over seven tons of victual supplies are carried in the keelboat, fresh stewed or roasted game would not only preserve these supplies for leaner days, but be much preferred over salt pork, hardtack or even bacon & beans.

The second day is clear with a strong flow from the southeast. Lewis is pleased with this luck and orders the sail hoisted to catch the wind and propel the keelboat upriver at more than 2 knots. He remarks to Clark. "If this breeze holds, we could make twenty miles today. We shall not put ashore for lunch, but take advantage of every hour of winds. I believe that the pirogues will be able to keep up."

As the little fleet advances up the river, Drouillard, scouting and hunting again, hastens to keep ahead cross country. He is somewhat less careful to follow well-established game trails as he hurries to scout ahead of the "fleet". A misplaced step ruins his day. "God damn it all to hell!" He screams as the rattlesnake retracts its fangs and attempts another strike. Drouillard pivots the scattergun in his right hand and lets go with a full blast of heavy bird shot. With presence of mind he drops the scattergun, and pulls his heavy knife in one flowing motion. He severs the snake' head, scans the area for another snake, only then sits down, unwinds his leather legging exposing the fang marks. He then slashes the bite diagonally between the fang marks. Painfully he presses the flesh of the wound together, thereby causing it to bleed profusely. He hopes that enough venom may be extricated in order to somewhat lessen the effects of the bite. After this primitive extraction, he fires his Hawkins rifle in successions, a pre-arranged signal of warning and for help. Douillard then pauses to consider whether he should sit quietly and await assistance or limp down the bluff toward the river. As he considers his course of action, he examines the wound. It seems that his leggings did stop the snake's fangs from deeply penetrating his leg. His swift, self-aid action, most likely extricated most of the venom. For being unlucky, he is lucky today. He stands up, fires his Hawkins into the air and begins to descend the bluff toward the river. Lewis, on the bow of the Keelboat hears but cannot yet see Douillard. He scans the bluff for Douillard and curses this time-consuming luck! "Turn in. Beach the boat". Lewis commands in a loud, but disgusted voice. "Run the God damned boat ashore. Captain Clark, prepare an armed shore party. Go find Drouillard!"

It isn't long before Clark's shore party comes face to face with the expedition's scout/hunter Drouillard as he is found limping his way toward the river. Clark inspects the wound. The fang marks are evident, the limb swollen but it seems that Drouillard's overzealous slashing of his leg is the worst of the matter. The party relieves Drouillard of his weapons and forage pouch as he is assisted back to the boat. Upon reaching the keelboat, Clark gets out the medicine chest, a chest stocked with numerous remedies, many of which were recommended to Captain Lewis by Dr. Benjamin Rush of Philadelphia, an acquaintance made to Lewis by the President himself.

Ammonia is the standard snake bite remedy, so Clark extracts a small bottle of ammonia and pours a quantity onto the wound. Drouillard grimaces in pain. The wound is wrapped and Drouillard finds himself a comfortable spot on the foredeck where he can rest, leg raised, and watch the scenery pass by for, at least, the remainder of the day.

"Push off." Commands Lewis. Lewis removes his large "portable clock" from its protective leather pouch. He notes the time and correlates it to the sun above, 1330. He surmises that the expedition as lost one hour and forty minutes to a snake. There will be no game for dinner tonight, but there will be snake stew, a small consolation.

May 15, 1804 – Monsieur Drouillard snake bit. Ate his assailant for supper. The Capt'n disappointed with the bad luck and lack of progress today. Charles Floyd.

Day 3 begins with reveille, breakfast and manning the boats. Private William Bratton, a Kentuckian, early volunteer, gunsmith and hunter is substituted for Drouillard as scout and hunter along the bluffs. He is pleased to be relieved of the back-breaking monotony aboard the keelboat and to be back in his element, hunting, even if it is hunting lightly wooded, open spaces, so very much unlike heavily wooded Kentucky. Bratton is pleased with his temporary duty.

After only three days, the men are finding the Missouri to be a tough customer indeed. The swift 5 knot current is a formidable obstacle even without a heavily laden keelboat yet the keelboat carries only a portion of the supplies that will be required of the journey. Some of the men are just now beginning to understand the physical hardships which lie ahead. During supper, insulated by the distraction of Private Pierre Cruzatte sawing on his fiddle, Privates Collins, Hall and Werner discuss an alternative plan.

"We always keep to the east side of the river. It wouldn't be difficult for a man to slip the picket at night and be far enough cross the prairie by breakfast that they give up on us." Offers Collins to his messmates.

"Supposing you are right, it can't be more than two or three day walk back to the Mississippi, then St Louis. By the time they get back, if'n they ever get back, we'll be long gone and forgotten. I'm in. Werner? "Ja, me too. I'm already tired of Ordway and poling the boat. I need a beer, some beef and a dirne." Adds Werner. "It's decided then, tomorrow". Finishes Collins. "Tomorrow then. I'll lift a rifle and a brace of pistols, powder and shot. Hall, you grab us a side of bacon, hard tack and a plug or two of tobacco. Werner, you get the prize, a flask of whiskey each, that should do us."

The following day is much the same as the preceding three days, row, pole and fight the Missouri, at least the weather is holding. In the late afternoon, the expedition puts ashore, makes camp and prepares the evening meal. Private Bratton was lucky today and bagged a whitetail. Fresh roasted venison, johnny cakes and a ration of liquor puts a smile on all, that is most of the men. The three conspirators are subdued in their comments tonight, smile a little, watch and wait for Cruzatte to tire of fiddling and for the men to bed down. The picket is posted, but the watch has slackened some, not having seen sign nor print of ferocious beast or aborigine. There is some comfort in the fact that they continue to bivouac on the east side of the river and have not yet reached the last know white settlement in these parts. The hamlet of Charette should stand about 50 miles upriver on the north side. A small gathering of seven or eight houses, but a known and friendly settlement nevertheless. Lewis plans to overnight there.

As the fires are reduced to embers and the men begin to slumber after a full day of exertion, a hardy meal and a ration of liquor, the three grab the pilfered provisions and slip out past the watch and into the night. By morning's reveille the missing men are noted.

"Sergeant Ordway reporting as ordered, sir!"

"Who's missing, sergeant?" Asks Clark.

"Three, sir. Privates Collins, Hart and Werner. Some few supplies as well." Responds Ordway.

"Very well. Dispatch Bratton and two others. Bring them back, preferably alive." Orders Clark.

"Sir, yes sir."

The three deserters have not travelled far, nor have they taken any precautions to cover their trace. They too were tired from the previous day's exertions, ate and drank more than usual, thinking that this would carry them farther in their escape. In fact, the fatigue and full bellies just slowed them down, and after a few miles of thrashing about in the dark, they laid out their blanket rolls and slept. The group had no compass, and were not adept in reading the stars, so without geographic references they had actually circled to the southeast and back toward the river. They had only distanced themselves a mere three miles from the expedition's encampment.

Note: 45) – Dirne, Gr, Sporting girl

Sergeant Ordway's discipline already forgotten, the three sleep until the sun is shining in their eyes. They stir, wake and start a small fire for breakfast. Private Bratton smells the smoke in the air even before seeing it. The three would be escapees are surrounded by their pursuers even before breakfast is finished. Hart hears Bratton's group first and reaches for a pistol as Bratton comes into full view.

"Don't make it worst for yourselves, lads." Barks Bratton while he and his fellow guards aim their rifles at the group.

"I shouldn't want to put a hole in you, Hart. But I will. Push that pistol away from you. Now, all of you, down on your knees, hands in the air. One more warning, any movement and I'll push daylight through you." Threatens Bratton.

The deserters are bound, tethered together and marched back to camp, to Sergeant's Ordway's ire and Captain Lewis' wrath.

May 17, 1804 – Captain Lewis called an assembly of the company, pickets and Corporal of the Guard excepted. Captain Lewis then explained to the assembled company that a Summary Court Martial would be held in accordance with Army regulations, he presiding as judge. I was chosen to prosecute Collins, Hart and Werner, the three deserters and Captain Clark would defend. I found it strange that the Captain would include the civilians in the assembly but I suppose that he was intending to make an example for all hands, soldiers and civilians alike.

Private Collins confessed to being the prime conspirator, making my task much easier. Of course, there are cases when someone will confess to the crimes of others in order to save their associates, but I didn't find this to be the case with Collins. Privates Hart and Werner had indeed deserted and pilfered stores, to which they also confessed.

Private Collins was then charged with Conspiracy, Desertion and Theft. The penalty for Desertion in times of war can be death, but good luck for Collins, the United States is not at war. As the appointed defender, Captain Clark did not dispute the confessions and findings of fact. He simply stated that the men, though volunteers, had not expected such arduous physical labor, were tired and just wanted to go home. They had stolen only enough supplies to sustain them until they could return to the Mississippi and then seek assistance from some sympathetic persons along the way. He asked the court to be lenient as this was their collective first offense. I countered this argument by saying that their act of desertion had hurt the morale and endangered the entire company and the mission. I did concede this as being their first offense, but demanded punishment sufficient to deter future bad behavior. Both Captain Clark and I rested our cases within an hour.

Captain Lewis had written some notes, reviewed these, then seemed to survey all the faces of the assembled company, only then did he speak. I quote him, "Privates Collins, Hart and Werner stand for your sentencing. Privates Hart and Werner, you have been found guilty of desertion and theft. I sentence you to 20 lashes each. Execution of sentence is suspended for remainder of the expedition. Should either of you dare to violate my trust again, this sentence with be carried out in conjunction with any other punishment the court may sentence you for said future infraction or infractions. Do you understand?" Both Hart and Werner sheepishly acknowledged Captain Lewis' order.

Then Captain Lewis turned to Private Collins. "Private Collins, you are the confessed instigator of this debacle. I find you guilty of conspiracy, desertion and theft. You seem to be that proverbial "rotten apple" in the barrel. Well, this court will not tolerate your bad attitude inflecting others of the company. I sentence you to 50 lashes. Execution of this sentence will be carried out immediately. In that you have confessed, there are no grounds for appeal. Unless of course, you have lied to the court. Have you lied to the court Private Collins?" Collins shook his head and mumbled no, sir. Captain Lewis then continued. "I consider this court's sentence of 50 lashes to be lenient. I could have you shot. Do you understand that lad? I could clap you in irons and send you back to St Louis to be held until we return, only then having a hearing and rendering a judgement. But no, this court wishes that this sad episode of irresponsible behavior to dealt with and put behind

Private Collins is then taken to the keelboat where he is tied around the mast. His shirt had been removed and a mask placed over his eyes. Neither Captain Lewis nor Captain Clark had brought a cat o' nine tails, so Sergeant Ordway improvised by cutting a willow switch from along the river bank. The good sergeant needs the man as well as the lesson, so he is prudent in his application, causing angry, red welts to Private Collins back but no lacerations. Collins' betrayal and stupidity have caused him no permanent harm but a lesson well remembered.

The company witnesses punishment. Generally, there is little sympathy for any of the deserters, Collins in particular. He is only getting what he deserves and lucky at that. One witness however sees the punishing lashes from a different point of view. York stands with the men witnessing punishment, but there is an aurora of terror in his eyes.

On the fifth day, Friday 18 May, 1804 the expedition continues their journey up the Missouri River, intermediate stop, La Charette, 50 miles from where they began.

The next week is uneventful, full of monotony but without the drama of snake bites and desertions. Monsieur Drouillard is recovered and back on the scout and hunting for the company's subsistence as the little fleet slowly makes its way up the river. Private Bratton is commended by Captain Lewis on his noteworthy contributions during Drouillard's convalesce and is rewarded by being promoted to permanent scout/hunter, working on equal terms with and independent of Drouillard. Both men are satisfied with the arrangement in that the company's survival is less dependent on any one person.

On May 25th 1804 the little fleet sights the hamlet of La Charette as it rounds a bend in the river. Captain Lewis orders the keelboat's bow gun to be fired as a salute, causing unintended and considerable alarm in the sleepy collection eight houses. Mother's gather their children and shutter windows and doors, as several curious boys run toward the sound of the gun to investigate. Only two men are presently in La Charette, a storekeeper and a trapper recovering from a misunderstanding with the Sioux.

The boys bound along the riverbank as Lewis' fleet approaches La Charette. The fear of danger subsiding, first windows then doors open revealing a friendly group of wives and children. Their men, mostly hunters or trappers are gone. The shopkeeper, a retired trapper named Catacus is the first of the adult population to wander down to the riverbank and greet the expedition. He is, of course, acting out of both curiosity and self-interest in seeking news from the world beyond La Charette and any potential sales, large or small.

"Bonjour Mes Messieurs, parlez-vous francais?" Catacus is being somewhat coy as Lewis has hoisted the Stars & Stripes over the keelboat, and he is well aware that he is dealing with English speaking Americans. But this IS French territory, after all.

"No, sir I speak only some French. I am Captain Meriwether Lewis of the United States. I am in command of this expedition of the Missouri and beyond. You, sir, are NOW a citizen of the United States of America. This territory has been sold to the United States by France.

Welcome, Citizen ....???

"Citizen Catacus, your honor. I too speak some English, but sometimes a little French also.

Note: 46) *Fr. Bonjour Mes Messieurs, parlez-vous francais?* Good day gentlemen, do you speak French?

Forgive me please for my lack of eloquence. So, I am no longer a *Francais?* We live in interesting times, *n'est-ce pas?* I am born in Pas de Calais in the Kingdom of France, a Frenchman but, of course, one of my ancestors, no doubt, may have slept with an English or even a Dutch woman or two. My king was Louis but then they say I am now a Republican, the Bourbon are *fini.* It is alright, I never liked that Austrian bitch anyhow. She suits me better *sans sa tete.* And now, here come *les Americans.* You confuse poor Catacus once again. I, no we, are now Americans? *C'est la vie.* Our village has little to offer you, sir. The husbands are trapping or hunting, there is only Phillipe and myself here to watch over the women and the childs. And Phillipe, well, he is not much so good now, a Sioux made coup with his head. He suffers much, but I expect he will get better. Better a tap on the head then an arrow up *le cul, n'est- ce pas?"*

"Yes, well Monsieur Catacus, we require very little. My company will bivouac here near the landing and may patronize your store for whatever you may have to offer; a little more tobacco, a keg or two of whiskey, something sweet perhaps. I have coin or if you prefer, we may barter with some trade goods from your store. Something attractive to the children or ladies?" Proffers Lewis. *"Excellent, Monsieur le Capitain.* I welcome you to La Charette.

Notes: 47) Fr., *Francais,* French., 48) Fr., *N'est-ce pas,* isn't that right? 49) Fr., *fini,* finished, 50) Fr., *sans sa tete,* without her head, 51) Fr., *C'est la vie,* that's life, 52) Fr., *le cul,* the ass

The following day's reveille is a difficult one for the company. The high social spirits and and far too much distilled spirits have transformed reveille into a contest of wills against aching heads and lethargy. Lewis desires to demonstrate a dignified, crisp, military-like departure from La Charette but has to be satisfied with an organized assemblage taking to the boats at departure. Fortunately for Captain Lewis' pride, the freshly-minted United States citizens of La Charette are slow this morning also, and only a few boys and Monsieur Catacus bid the company farewell.

As May, "The Planting Moon" becomes June, "The Strawberry Moon" the men settle into a routine. The days become warmer, and the river has begun to relax its spring flow, revealing more of itself and lessening its current. Navigation is not difficult but requires a keen eye and a Ruderman's steady hand.

Drouillard and Bratton also are becoming more adept at hunting the prairie. The bounty includes; prairie chicken, rabbit, deer and snake, all of which make for fine eating. Drouillard, more than Bratton, is becoming obsessed with bagging the fleet-footing antelope of the prairie.

The antelope are shy, making it difficult for Drouillard to get within range of his heavy, short barreled, .54 caliber Hawkins. He considers borrowing an elegant .40 caliber Kentucky long rifle. Effectively a blade-sighted Hawkins is good for 50-100 yards. The lighter Kentucky gun, given Douillard's skill, easily at 200 yards more. With a little extra powder charge and some good, ole-fashioned windage, he may yet be able to bag one of these buff-colored buggers yet!

Chapter 11

THE HUMAN BEINGS

The Oto-Missouria people, had like many other native tribes migrated to and fro in accordance with their relations and alliances, with their cultural evolution and, of course, due to their interactions with the white man. Descendant of Siouan people, by 1673, when the French explorer Jacques Marquette first notes their existence on a map, the Oto had adopted a semi-nomadic culture, living in substantial lodges, growing squash and beans, and occasionally taking up the tipi for a buffalo hunt. Some twenty years later *Chevalier d'Ordre de Saint Louis,* Pierre Le Moyne d'Iberville, a French noble, soldier and explorer whose brother founded New Orleans on behalf of the Sun King and himself, spends an extended period with people, the people who call themselves The Human Beings.

By the eighteenth century the fortunes of the Oto-Missouria had become greatly diminished due to incessant warfare with the Sacs and the Fox and migration pressures which had pushed them from their original Great Lakes region homeland. With the material benefit of interaction with the white man came the inevitable decline due to disease, both smallpox and venereal, alcohol, and the disruption of balanced cultural norms which had preserved these people for centuries. Regardless, on his third expedition of the Mississippi and Missouri watersheds, Chevalier d'Iberville takes advantage of the friendly curiosity of the Oto-Missouria and establishes a base camp near them as he works his survey. Interactions are natural between the whites and the natives. Iron goods, knives and cloth are in great demand and readily exchanged for information and hospitality. "A good trade."

By the year 1804 the Oto and Missouria tribes had amalgamated due to their reduced numbers. The combined tribe consisted of only about 250 people living on the along the west bank of the Missouri river in several small "towns". The Oto-Missouria oven-shaped, earth-covered lodges grouped in these towns distinguished them from other aboriginal people. Due to their proximity as one of the easternmost of the western tribes, the Oto and Missouria peoples have had infrequent but steady and increasing contact with white explorers, hunters and trappers. Any advantage gained by the tribes in the acquisition of valuable trade goods has been offset by alcohol and disease.

In early July, some two months and three hundred hard miles from the beginning of the expedition, Private Bratton, while scouting and hunting the western bank of the river comes upon the first of the Oto's seemingly abandoned villages. From a distance, Bratton sees what appears to be a collection of beaver or muskrat houses out of water. This doesn't make much sense to him, so he measures his pace, primes his piece and slowly moves forward to investigate. Carefully he moves up toward the first structure. Upon closer inspection he recognizes the strange structure to be a masterfully designed and built earthen lodge. After surveying the environs, he carefully pulls aside the animal hide which serves as the entrance closure and steps into the interior of the lodge. His eyes slowly adjusting from the brightness of the morning to the dimness of the lodge, Bratton is surprised at its spaciousness.

Notes: 53) Fr. *Chevalier d'Ordre de Saint Louis*, Knight of the Order of St. Louis, 54) Many Native Americans similarly described themselves as such, e.g. Comanche, the human beings, Cherokee, the real people, etc.

The floor is packed earth, its walls constructed out of logs and sticks covered with earth. Various utensils, baskets, woven cords, and paraphernalia are neatly stored around. He realizes that its former inhabitants have not abandoned this place. Most likely the natives are off hunting and would not be pleased to know that he was trespassing their lodge or village. Bratton decides that it prudent to leave, and report his findings to the Captain.

Excitedly Bratton picks up his pace in retracing his route back toward the little fleet slowly making its way up the river. He descends the steep embankment, discharges one shot and waves the boats to shore. Little does Bratton realize, his reconnaissance of the first of the Oto towns has not gone unnoticed. The tribe has left two boys, those yet uninitiated as hunter/warriors, but boys capable of living off the land without the daily support of the tribe and able to ride their ponies as if they were simply another appendage thereof. Little Calf and Throws Stones quietly exit the village as Bratton noisily entered. They circle to the west then back around behind Bratton just off the trace from whence he came. As Bratton excitedly retraces his path, the boys sit by quietly, watching then following him back to the river. As he descends the embankment, Little Calf and Throws Stones can see the little fleet as it makes its way toward shore and waiting Private Bratton. This is their first, and from the distance, impressive glance of white men. Once Bratton boards the Keelboat, the boys hurry to their tethered ponies, mount and ride west by southwest toward the Nibrathka and their people.

Some 100 miles to the west, the Oto are encamped on the Nibrathka or "flat" river (Platte), a crossroads for the herds of bison roaming the great prairie. The summer hunt is an essential season for the tribe, providing it with meat, dried in the hot prairie sun, hides, so painstakingly prepared by the women and bones, used in so many applications.

"Private Bratton reporting as ordered, sir."

"Yes, ok, get on with it Private." Orders an annoyed Lieutenant Clark.

"Natives, sir. I came upon a native settlement, 20, maybe 25 mud-stick lodges. It is unoccupied but in my opinion, sir, it has not been abandoned." Reports Bratton.

"Explain yourself, Bratton. Unoccupied but not abandoned? Queries Clark.

"Yes, sir. The village is unoccupied. No dogs, no ponies, no fires, no people. The settlement is in good condition however. I only inspected the interior of one lodge, but utensils, baskets and such were neatly stored. I expect they've gone off on a summer hunt." Explains Bratton.

"Good, clear report Bratton. You'll make Corporal someday. Keep up the good eye and good work.". Compliments Clark.

Clark turns his attention from Bratton and looks for Lewis. Not knowing exactly where Lewis is, he opens the door to the interior of the keelboat and calls.

"Captain Lewis, Captain Lewis, sir. We need to speak."

Lewis is below, writing in his journal and nursing a slight headache.

Even before Lieutenant Clark reports Bratton's discovery, Little Calf and Throws Stones have distanced themselves 5 miles from the little fleet. They slow their ponies to a canter and banter.

"We should have counted coup. He was so close" Exclaims Throws Stones.

"No, Little Thief and Big Horse would be angry with us. We were told only to watch and report. If we had counted coup on the white man, the other warriors would be angry too. We are not warriors yet, but we will be soon by following the words of Little Thief and Big Horse and reporting the presence of white men" Replies Little Calf.

"Maybe you are right. But that was probably the only chance we will ever get to counting coup on a white man. He was soooo close! Whins Throws Stones.

"Yes, but he had a rifle and a pistol. Maybe you would be dead now? Maybe I would be dead also? The presence of the white men would go unreported to Little Thief and Big Horse and the men of our village would mock us and be angry with us even in death!"

It takes two days for Little Calf and Throws Stones to find their people along the Nibrathka.

As the elder of the two, Little Calf reports first to, Little Thief, then moves on to find Big Horse.

The duo are congratulated by the Peace Chiefs and the warriors for having done well and followed instructions. Throws Stones accepts the accolades a bit sheepishly. Little Calf does not betray his friend.

Little Thief represents the Oto people, whereas Big Horse represents the Missouria of the combined band. Both Little Thief and Big Horse are Peace Chiefs, chosen to represent the band in times of peace. Presently, and hopefully the Oto-Missouria "will fight no more forever." It is decided to send a party back to the village immediately under the guidance of Little Thief. Big Horse will stay with the people until the hunt can be reasonably concluded. The hunt is too important to be prematurely ended, but a group of many white men in three boats is not be ignored either. Little Calf and Throws Stones have done their duty and are rewarded by being allowed to stay in camp and assist the hunters in finishing the Buffalo hunt. They are elated.

Little Thief has experienced white men before. They smell bad and are dirty. They drink whiskey too much, and try to sleep with the women, any woman. It is best to hide the young girls, women and female dogs when white men come to camp. Trading is the only use for white men. Also, stealing their mules and horses can be profitable, but dangerous. They become belligerent when they lose their mounts. They should not drink so much and sleep so soundly.

Note: 55) "I will fight no more forever." Chief Joseph, Nez Perce 1877

The prairie is a dangerous place! Little Thief entertains these thoughts as he and six other braves canter east toward the Missouri and the uninvited whites.

After hearing Bratton's report, Lewis tells Clark. "We will bivouac near the native village tonight, but on the opposite side of river. In this way, we'll have the river between us and the aborigines should they return from their hunt and should they be hostile. We'll also post more pickets tonight. Are you comfortable with this?"

"Yes, sir, I'm good with that." I am assuming that you want to take a walk through of the village tomorrow?" Queries Clark "Yes, of course. Given its temporary abandonment, it presents us with an opportunity to map the layout of the village, architecture and construction of their lodges, examine any paraphernalia, even take a look see at where they shit. Wonderful opportunity. In the morning I'll call a school circle of the company. Although the main body will stay with our vessels, those pickets and accompanying soldiers must understand that NOTHING shall be disturbed or pilfered. We are not Vandals, we are explorers. We shall explore the native village and leave it exactly as we find it. Please, William, if my words are not clearly understood, then say something to the men also. It is not a matter of military propriety, it is a matter of utmost importance."

"Understood Meriwether. I could not agree with you more. Indians are known for their light fingers, but really take issue with others taking their possessions. Doesn't make much sense to us, does it? Live by the sword, die by the sword, so to say. I think that it is a matter of pride.

They do not like to be seen as being vulnerable. If someone can steal from them, they are weak. If they steal from others, they are clever and strong. Do you agree?" Sophisizes Clark.

"Could be. It's always been a mystery to me too." Responds Lewis somewhat distracted.

Little Thief and his six braves rest only in consideration of their ponies. They cannot expect to steal fresh ponies from a remuda, these whites have come by canoe and some type of floating lodge. They canter, they walk, then they canter again. It will take two full days to reach the first town, the place where Little Calf and Throws Stones spotted them first. On the third day after having heard the news of the white men, Little Thief stops the group just beyond the western horizon of the town. One brave will tend the ponies, Little Thief and the five others will approach.

From their vantage points Little Thief can see no sign of occupation; no smoke, no noise, no movement. He and his braves move closer, always taking advantage of natural cover. They reach the town and find it undisturbed and unoccupied. Peering over the bluff and viewing both sides of the river, they see no canoes, no white men and no floating lodge. The white men are gone.

Little Thief now holds counsel with his braves. "The whites are gone. Should we follow them or should we go back to our hunt?" Asks Little Thief of the group. No one is now concerned with the hunt.

"We should pursue them." Says the youngest, the horse-tender brave.

"No, we should circle around to the west and position ourselves between here and the next town. Let the white men discover us. It may be easier to discern their intentions if they come across a few of us simply hunting or fishing along the river. Let them think that THEY found us." Says Little Thief after thinking the question through. He also decides to send one brave back to Big Horse to explain what he has decided to do.

"Go. Go tell Big Horse that the white men have seemingly not disturbed the town and that they are gone. We will go upriver and meet them somewhere between the two towns. If they have turned again down river, then, they are gone – for now. If we meet and parley with the whites, then we will try to keep them talking until you return from the hunt. These are the words of Little Thief."

The distance to the next Oto-Missouria town is but a day's, then some walk. A fleet hunter can make the trek in *giizhig-oon*[57], one day. The women, children and those advanced in years longer. On the river in the heavy-laden keelboat and pirogues, it takes longer, perhaps four days depending on the winds although with the ending of July, the currents are abated and much progress is being made. Private Bratton had not yet discovered the second of the Oto-Missouria towns when first his nose then his sharp hunter's eyes catch something a mile or so distant. Unbeknownst to Bratton the hunter/scout, Little Thief has baited him with a healthy campfire and roasting meat. Bratton does not have to visually acquire Little Thief's band, he already knows what is there, a hunting party. Bratton turns heel and scurries back again, back to the little fleet laboriously making its way up the Missouri.

Once again Bratton fires a signal shot. The warning is picked-up by the men on the boats, But, also Little Thief, who knows that his trap has been sprung. He will treat with the white men tomorrow.

"Smoke Captain Lewis, smoke and movement north. I come back bout a mile. I expect the injuns to be bout a mile further on. No settlement that I saw, just smoke and some movement." Reports Private Bratton.

"Well, could be a hunting party or possibly we are coming up upon another settlement.

Don't rightly know which. Expecting we'll soon find out. I'll report to Captain Lewis. Thank you, Private." Concludes Clark.

Without the knowledge of knowing that the expedition is being watched, Lewis, Clark, the little fleet and the scouts continue up the river and with their daily duties as in the weeks before. They have concluded that these particular indigenous people are off hunting and will not return until the hunt is successfully concluded and their gardens are ready for harvest, maybe a month yet. They are perhaps more vigilant than before but nothing more.

Note: 57) Ojibwe *giizhig-oon,* a day

July 27th 1804 – The vast western sky, the seemingly endless prairie of grass, the heavily wooded river vales all give one the sensation of emptiness, yet we know native people are there – somewhere - and living creatures of every kind inhabit every rock, crevice, wood and field. The river is alive with fish, frogs and crawdad. The presence of God, Creator of Heaven and Earth is palpable. Charles Floyd.

Little Thief and his five warriors have flanked the expedition on their ponies. One brave watches the little fleet from a position just to the rear of the hunter/scouts, Bratton and Drouillard, who are now both working the western bank of the river. They scan the horizon, open their nostrils and seek sign, but are not inclined to look behind themselves on the very ground so recently tread upon. Drouillard makes a poignant observation.

"You know Bratton, the scarcity of the game these past few days is beginning to bother me.

Track is everywhere, but game is not. Sure, the Indian village may have hunted the area down some, but they are gone, and the track is here, yet there is not any game save a few partridge and chicken. I find this strange."

"As do I. It tells me that the people of the village are not as far away as we may want to believe. Better keep a sharp eye out. I feel it." Agrees Bratton.

The very next day, first Drouillard, then Bratton catch the scent of camp smoke in the air.

They habitually prime and safety lock their pieces, glance at each other and move forward at a careful, measured pace. Their hands grip the rifles hard, some small sweat begins to build on the stocks and their hearts beat at a more rapid rate. They are sure of what lies ahead but unsure of just what lies ahead.

Little Thief places some more wood on his "signal" fire concealing his purpose as if only smoking some fish on a willow rack. Bratton can see the large filets of fish as the Indians sit around eating its small, black eggs and talking animatedly. Little Thief feigns surprise and rises pointing out the two white scouts to his braves. They all rise but purposefully do not arm themselves, the scout find this out of character.

Bratton and Drouillard continue to advance but do not change their "weapons at the ready" stance. Little Thief is disarmingly friendly, gesturing then speaking in French.

"*Bonjour mes freres. Comment sa va?*"

"*Nous sommes bien mes freres. Nous ne voudront pas vous deranger mes freres.*" Greets Drouillard in reply.

"*Mangez, mangez.*" Says Little Thief proffering some of the caviar of sturgeon.

The scouts squat, Indian style, and eat some of the odd, little black eggs. They find these surprisingly delicious, but are unnerved by these overly friendly and accommodating natives.

Both Bratton and Drouillard never relinquish their weapons and continually look around and behind themselves.

A mile or so downstream, the little fleet slowly advances up the river. Bratton, speaking no French, manages to excuse himself from the *parley* and returns to advise Captain Lewis of the encounter. Drouillard continues to talk, eat and enjoy the apparent hospitality of Little Thief.

Once clear of the gathering, down over the embankment and on the river bank, Bratton fires his rifle into the air and waves the little fleet in.

"Private Bratton reporting, sir. Drouillard and I came upon five Indians in a camp about a mile distant. They are, that is they were, smoking fish and eating. Very friendly for a hunting party, for any party for that matter, just sitting around as if they were expecting us." Reports Bratton in an uncharacteristically excited manner.

Notes: 58) Fr., Bonjour mes freres. Comment sa va? Good morning my brothers. How are you? 59) Fr., Nous sommes bien mes freres. Nous ne voudront pas vous deranger mes freres. We are fine my brothers. We do not wish to disturb you, my brothers. 60) Fr., Mangez. Eat.

"Very good, Private. A mile distant you say? Five warriors?" Queries Clark.

"Yes, bout a mile, sir. Five Indians, but only one did any talking. Maybe he was the chief? I don't know. This one, he speaks French. Drouillard is still up there with them. He seems to be having a good time, eating, talking and all." Further explains Bratton.

"Very good, Bratton. Thank you." Concludes Clark.

"Sergeant Ordway, if you please." Calls Clark Ordway hurries to Lieutenant Clark.

"Have the boatmen put ashore on the east bank about a half mile up. Assemble a squad of six men, cleaned-up and in uniform. We will take one pirogue across with some gifts and see just what we've got here. Hopefully Drouillard is still wearing his topknot. You come also, we'll leave Sergeant Floyd in charge" Orders Clark.

Lieutenant Clark then leaves the deck and goes below, knocks then enters Captain Lewis' cabin.

"Well, Meriwether, it appears that we've come upon our first aborigines. Bratton and Drouillard stumbled upon a small hunting, or fishing party as it were. Bratton just reported. Drouillard is still having *parley* with the Indians. I've ordered the boats ashore on the opposite bank and am assembling a shore party. Do you wish to lead it? I can remain here with the men?" Asks Clark.

"Very good, William. Yes, I would like to lead the party, if you have no objection?" Says Lewis.

"None at all, Meriwether. Ah, just one more thing. Bratton says that the Indians were in camp, eating, smoking fish – as though they were expecting us. I find this a little strange?" Adds Clark. "Hmmm, Maybe they were watching over their village after all? That wouldn't surprise me.

As you mentioned, Indians are loath to lose what belongs to them. Let us go and treat with these Red Sticks." Adds Lewis.

After discharging Bratton, one pirogue, unloaded of its supplies and with a skeleton crew are send back across to the western bank of the river to wait for Drouillard. Its four men are armed and vigilant but not expecting trouble. Their wait may be lengthy however, as Drouillard is by nature a talker, as can be Indians who want something. In the meanwhile, Lewis carefully prepares his uniform and gifts. He wants to make a sterling impression on the "children" of the Great White Father.

"Sergeant Ordway, make certain that our men are inspection ready to treat with the Indians. I wish to make a first class impression upon them. I want brushed uniforms and belts, polished brass, trimmed hair and beards. We'll take York along with us. Let's give them something to look at. My orders stand for York also, pretty as goin to Sunday Services.

It is near dark before Drouillard shows up to where the pirogue is beached. The crew takes him aboard and quickly paddles across the river to camp where their supper is waiting.

Drouillard is not particularly hungry having smoked and eaten with Little Thief all afternoon.

Lewis is eager to question Drouillard before meeting with Little Thief himself.

Little Thief is disappointed in the day. True, the white men did fall for his ruse and he spent a leisurely afternoon smoking and talking with the Frenchman, but this Frenchman is no different than any of the other Frenchmen he had met before. Perhaps tomorrow will bear better fruit.

August 3, 1804 – Our hunter/guides Private Bratton and George Drouillard treated with aborigines today. Captain Lewis and a squad of men are to go across the river in the morning and treat with them. Both Bratton and Drouillard report the Injuns to be friendly ones. Everyone is relieved. We'd like not to engage any hostiles. Charles Floyd

Now that the expedition is certain that they are being observed, Captain Lewis makes a ceremony for the hidden Indians to watch. Reveille is called by bugle, not just Sergeant Ordway's boot. The men are assembled and inspected prior to breakfast. A big breakfast is served after which Captain Lewis and his squad board a pirogue with a small box of gifts and sporting a large American flag at its bow. Since departing Camp Du Bois, Lewis has been concerned about the quantity and quality of the gifts which he is bearing. Today he has chosen; knives, tobacco, vermilion face paint and one shiny, silver Peace Medal for the chief. These should be perfect for a hunting or as it may be, a spying party. The river is soon crossed and Lewis leads his men up the embankment and to the "fish camp" of Little Thief.

Little Thief rises and gestures as he sees the small group of white men arriving. Captain Lewis leads the shore party, followed by Sergeant Ordway, a flag bearer, M. Drouillard, four privates and York. As Lewis had predicted, he has seized the initiative away from Little Thief by including York. The Indians are visibly awed by the large, black man and his fuzzy hair. More than once in the first few moments, Drouillard overhears the word *mashkodebizhiki niiyaw* or buffalo man. The chief and his warriors are impressed. Little Thief's eyes turn from York back to Lewis, then shifting from Lewis to Drouillard and back to Lewis again. The party is invited to sit and eat.

Lewis orders the men to sit, except for the flag bearer, he will stand holding the national ensign throughout the parley. Lewis has a box placed in front of him and opened. The Indians strain to look inside the box, but Lewis makes them wait.

"In the name of the Great White Father Jefferson, greetings. We come in peace. We travel the Missouri river to meet the peoples here and to study the land, animals and plants. As evidence of our intentions, we bring the Great White Father's children gifts, gifts from our cities in the east." Announces Lewis.

Lewis reaches into the box and removes a plug of tobacco. He then reaches down and slowly pulls a tomahawk from his belt. This tomahawk is utilitarian but sports a bowl on one end and has a hollow tubed handle. It can be used for either chopping or smoking, most likely smoking.

Lewis charges the bowl and lights the strange pipe. He makes one or two dramatic draws then hands the pipe to Little Thief. Little Thief accepts the pipe, smokes, then passes the pipe around. A good sign. For a while the group of white explorers and native red men sit smoking, thinking and occasionally eating. Each group had its own motivations for this parley. Little Thief is there to protect the band's towns, possessions and to understand who these white intruders are and what they may want. It was natural that visitors of good intentions should bear gifts, so Little Thief did have this expectation. He is annoyed however with Lewis' verboseness, and talk of a Great White Father. The Oto-Missouria have no Great White Father and most certainly are not the needy children of white men, whoever they are and from wherever they come. He held these feeling deep within his breast so as not to arouse his warriors.

As the time for the parley comes to an end, Lewis orders the gifts to be distributed; each warrior received a shiny, new hunting knife, a small tin of red face paint, and some tobacco. As chief, Little Thief receives these things and in addition the tomahawk pipe and a silver peace medal from President Thomas Jefferson, the Great White Father. Little Thief is satisfied, but not overly impressed with Lewis' generosity. What had he expected, he himself is not certain, but a rifle would have fine gift. A rifle gift however, would have presented yet another problem, as to how to reciprocate in kind. These explorers don't seem the types to need temporary wives and any such available Oto squaws are one hundred miles west on the Nibrathka drying meat, and processing buffalo hides.

Final "good byes" are made and the men of two worlds continue in their respective orbits; Lewis and the shore party return to their boats as Little Thief breaks camp to continue north to the third of the Oto-Missouria towns where he will wait for Big Horse and the band. Little Thief will meet the overly proud white man and his followers again soon, sooner than they may have expected. Lewis too contemplates on the day and all that was "not" said this day! Lewis looks forward to penning in his journal tonight, a day of consequence, a day to be remembered as his first glance at the legendary Plains tribes.

August 4, 1804 – The Capt'en met with a small party of Injuns today. He says they are of the Oto-Missouria band which lives in several "towns" along the Missouri River. They seem peaceful enough, and like all Injuns, they love to smoke and talk. They seemed impressed by York. The Capt'en planned that one! The main bunch is off on a Buffalo hunt somewhere on the plains west of here. They are expected back soon. Curious to see what their squaws look like? Charles Floyd.

Several days later, the expedition meets up with Big Horse and the main band returning from the hunt. Lewis is disappointed in this second meeting with the Oto-Missouria. He brings additional gifts for the wives and the band, such as a brass kettle, a looking glass, beads and cloth. Big Horse quickly passes these trinkets to others and is unimpressed with his knife and Peace medal. He warns Lewis that the Sioux are more difficult than he and Little Thief. They should watch their top knots!

After the *parley* with Big Horse, the expedition continues up the river. There is a southeast breeze, the river courses straight, the current steady but having slackened along with summer's flow. The warm days and cooperative river make for progress and good humor. In the back of each mind however are thoughts of the Lakota who often encamp near the falls not far ahead.

August 17, 1804 – Today was a fine day, much progress has been made. The men are in high spirits but quietly discuss the Lakota who wander this region. I am a little off color today. A slight fever and pain in my side. I suppose I ate

Captain Lewis and Lieutenant Clark are concerned about Sergeant Floyd's sweats and pale appearance. He tries to assure them, but his assurances are weak. The next day the expedition encamps on the east bank of the river as to offer some protection from the expected appearance of the Lakota. They minister to Sergeant Floyd, their favorite. He was one of the first to volunteer for the mission, is a fine, muscled specimen of a man, intelligent and literate. But with each hour the good Sergeant's condition grows worse. He is now is great distress.

Lewis, Clark, his fellow non-commissioned officers and the men, each assess his chances for survival, it seems that only the hour is unknown.

On August 19th Sergeant Floyd rallies, much to the surprise and delight of all. He sits, talks some and sips soup broth. Lewis orders a warm bath prepared for his refreshment. Then, suddenly his condition worsens. He calls for his captain. Lewis arrives promptly.

"Captain, dear captain, I am going away. Please write a letter for me, and tell my kin that I was a good soldier and served all well." Whispers Floyd. He presses his precious journal into Lewis' hand and passes from caring.

Although half expected for these past few days, Sergeant Charles Floyd dies on August 20th 1804. Captain Lewis and Lieutenant Clark order the "ship's" carpenter to make a simple coffin into which the bathed and uniformed body of the late sergeant is placed. The company is assembled, good words are offered in tribute and in prayer. The sergeant's body and coffin are then lowered into a grave, a grave high above the river on a bluff, a bluff thenceforth known as Floyd's Bluff. May he rest in peace.

Captain Lewis is driven, driven to complete the mission to the best of his abilities and to serve his master, The President. Lieutenant Clark however, as Second In Command, Adjutant, and Quartermaster is acutely concerned with logistics and the welfare of the company in order to support that mission. The tragic loss of the good sergeant hits Clark hard as he had privately hoped that with proper planning and execution of those plans, all might survive the expedition.

"How many more will die?" Clark questions himself. How might he better ameliorate the company's chances through better planning? Clark ponders these questions as Captain Lewis opens Floyd's journal and begins to write.

August 20, 1804 – This is the last entry in the journal of Sergeant Charles Floyd, Corps of Discovery, United States Army. Sergeant Floyd passed this day into the hands of his Creator. His mortal remains have been buried with all honor on a handsome bluff on the eastern bank of the Missouri River, Louisiana Territory in the proximity of the Oto-Missouria townships. May he rejoice in the eternal and loving presence of his risen Lord. Captain Meriwether Lewis.

With heavy hearts the expedition breaks camp and gets underway. It is late summer now and Meriwether ponders the fall season, be it an early winter or an Indian summer. He hopes to drive the little fleet some five-six hundred miles still before making winter camp. Whether this goal is possible or not will depend much on the weather, native tribes and geography.

Lewis is informed that semi-hostile plain tribes, the Lakota, claim the lands between the Oto-Missouria and the Mandan. The Oto and Mandan are considered friendly, but the Lakota are not to be trusted. Lewis calculates to be in proximity of the Mandan by December, hopefully the winter will not be early or severe.

Lewis calculates a distance of one hundred or more miles from Floyd's Bluff to a fork in the river. The fork is comprised of the Missouri and a tributary, the *Tehankasandata,* where there is said to be cascading falls over a bedrock of pink granite. Lakota and Dakota tribes often are present in the place as are their numerous burial mounds. The river is turbulent there, and portage difficult due to bluffs. A known but unknown mystery, as is much of this expedition.

Lewis intends to discuss the matter with Clark, but the unknown factors make planning a superfluous notion.

September 1, 1804 – I have maintained a comprehensive journal during this expedition. The journal notes the flora, fauna, topography and aboriginal peoples of this land. Until this moment however I have not made mention of my personal feelings, even in interceding between York and Clark. Since Sergeant Floyd's passing, a dark cloud of despair has come over me. Grieving yes, but yet more. The scope of this venture is overwhelming. The land and its people are hard. We have come to know more about the Missouri River, but the unknown presence of the Sioux is a constant worry. Beneath each rock a venomous snake, a biting spider, there are howling storms across the prairie. What when these storms turn to blizzards? Will I find Jefferson's Northwest Passage to the Orient or does it not exist? Am I chasing an enigma? Will I find the furry pachyderm or the ape-man giant? Or will the untamed Sioux end our great expedition in a flurry of lance and arrows? This burden is great. Am I enough of a man to lead it? Why Sergeant Floyd? He was a favorite. His raw enthusiasm was a pillar of strength. He was a light up your smoke and a quick wit. Now all that was him is lost. He molders under the prairie. Who will be next? Captain Meriwether Lewis.

As Lewis finishes penning his thoughts there is a great commotion, first on the port side of the keelboat, then aft. Lewis rushes out of his cabin to see a member of the crew thrashing in water mid-stream behind the boat.

"A poleman lost his balance, went overboard and is being swept away with the current, sir" Reports Sergeant Ordway. "The pirogues are starboard of the keelboat and missed him, sir."

Note: 61) Lakota, *Tehankasandata*, Big Sioux River

Before Lewis can react or even reply to Ordway there is another whoosh and geyser of water. Seaman, Lewis's great Labrador has taken to the water and paddles toward the unhappy, drowning poleman. Without hesitancy the huge dog swims to the distressed man and assists him to the shore. To the astonishment of all, Seaman has saved the poleman and jolted Lewis' consciousness to the present.

The boats ground ashore and the poleman Private is retrieved, now escorted by Seaman.

The men praise and congratulate Seaman, almost forgetting about the wet, cold and unhappy poleman Private.

"So, what happened Private Willard?" Questions Lewis.

"Asleep, sir. I must hav' nodded off then lost my balance on the pole. The next thing I knowd, I was in the water". Admits Willard "You were lucky Willard. Seaman is blind to your faults. I might have left you to the fishes.Snaps Lewis. "Change out of your wet clothes and get back to your post before I decide that your near drowning is not enough punishment for you. Any other company commander would see you whipped for falling asleep on duty. Get out of my sight, Private." Orders Lewis.

The next few day are uneventful. Hunters Drouillard and Bratton begin to see sign however.

The falls and the Sioux cannot be far ahead. An alert tension pervades the company. The hunters watch for fresh sign by day and the guard is doubled by night. Arms are at the ready.

Some day or two before the falls, Drouillard gives Bratton a sign, then doubles back, descends the bluff to the shoreline and waves in a pirogue. Drouillard boards the big canoe and order its occupants to catch up with the keelboat. Hardened arms, chest and backs dig into the river with their paddles and with practiced rhythm soon come alongside the keelboat, where big, bulky Drouillard is assisted aboard.

"The Capt'n please." Requests Drouillard of Sergeant Ordway.

"What is it, Drouillard?" Asks Ordway.

"Sign. Fresh sign and not a small party. Expect we'll be face to face with the Sioux plenty soon." States Drouillard flatly and without emotion.

CHAPTER 12

LAND OF THE LAKOTA

Old Chief Smoke is a young man as principal chief of the Oglala Sioux. At 29 years of age, he has already learned much in life, both from his elders and through experience. He knows that to the north of the Oglala are the Assinibone, to the east the Ojibwe, to the south the Kiowa, and to the far west, near the great mountains are the Shoshone. He knows these to be lustful tribes, lustful of Sioux ponies, Sioux women and Sioux hunting grounds. Old Chief Smoke's people perceive the pressure of change even now. Enemies in every direction of the wind, a bountiful but harsh and unforgiving environment, yet it is the whites who concern him most.

He knows the ways of his enemies, he understands the habits of his prey, he has learned to accept the extremes of his environment, yet it is the whites, though still few in number, who like a pest of insects or a prairie fire, few or small in the beginning, grow to a great, all-consuming conflagration in the end. He feels in his heart of hearts that it will be the white who represent the greatest of threats to his people.

In spite of his inner misgivings, he has reluctantly treated and traded with the French, and done no harm to the occasional passerby. But it is reported by runner that a company of these white creatures even now ascend the Missouri in a floating lodge accompanied by large canoes.

These whites number as many as able-bodied warriors in his tribe, armed with weapons of iron and wood.

Old Smoke Chief gathers the elders and leading warriors in his lodge. They talk, and smoke, and smoke and talk for many hours. It is finally agreed that Old Smoke Chief should go, accompanied by several warriors and one of the elders to meet and treat with these whites.

They should come to know what the whites want and where and when they will go. Prayers are offered, preparations made and Old Smoke Chief rides toward the river for a *parley.*

Old Smoke Chief's main village is a half day's ride west of the Missouri. He can gather a few better than sixty warriors at any given time. Women, children and the old number about two and a half times that many, amounting to a few more than two hundred souls in seventy lodges. This represents a strong number for protection but a burdenous number to feed.

The village is blessed with a pious medicine man and many strong, knowledgeable women, who care for new mothers, brew healing teas for sick children and minister to the aged. The women know that they too will grow old quickly for in addition to these duties they must; maintain the lodges, prepare meat and hides, make bone tools and clothing as well as rear their own young. The Lakota women are the bone and sinew of Lakota society. Without such women, Old Smoke Chief's band would melt away like the snow in spring.

Wearing their finest clothes and regalia, Old Smoke Chief's party rides east toward the river and the junction of the falls. There on the western bank of the river he will camp and wait for these whites. What he will say or how he will say it, he does not know yet. The attitude of these whites will dictate his words and actions, with the help of the Great Spirit and his ancestors.

The early September weather is fair so the warriors accompanying Old Smoke Chief are thoroughly enjoying the leisurely ride and camping along the river. Some light lodges are assembled using willow branches, foliage and leaves. Some fish are caught and lightly smoked, providing a welcome change to an otherwise monotonous diet of roasted game or the occasional dog.

Summers give way to fall early on the Plains. In the morning, on this 11th day of September, year of our Lord 1804, the surface of the river is eerily shrouded in a fog rising as vapors. As morning's sun rays cast light on the shadows, the Corp's pickets see two Lakota warriors astride their ponies in plain view on the western bank of the river. The warriors patiently wait to be clearly seen, then move north along the bluff in an invitingly slow manner. No sign is exchanged, but the message is clear – follow!

"So, what shall we do, Meriwether?" Questions Clark "We shall accept the Lakota invitation – on our terms! Fire the swivel gun in salute. Have reveille sounded, then call the company to assembly." Orders Lewis.

All within fifteen minutes, the swivel gun is fired, without projectile, and the bugler sound first; reveille then assembly. Lewis addresses the men.

"Men, this morning we shall meet the much -feared Lakota, the light cavalry of the Plains. He is watching this assembly, from there on the bluff, if in the event, you may have missed seeing him. We shall breakfast, break camp and follow the emissary up the river. I can't expect them to be far. Wear your best uniform, oil your leather and polish your brass. We want to make a proper impression. That is all. Sergeant Ordway, dismiss the men." Concludes Lewis.

Per Captain Lewis orders, the company prepares to meet the Sioux. They do not hasten the pace rather prepare, mess, break camp and load the vessels. The watching Lakota are unimpressed with the whites seeming inability to do things quickly. To the warriors everything is moving in slow motion. Are these whites so dull of brain?

Two Tongues watches and wonders just how the coming *parley* will play out. He has traded with the French many times but they travel alone or at most in a group of two or three. He has made a great effort, at the behest of the elders to learn some of their language so as to give the band some advantage over them.

I expect that we will finally encounter the Lakota on the morrow. I have so ordered preparations be made. The men have removed their oilskin packs from the keelboat and are brushing wool, shining brass and polishing leather even as I write these notes. We wish to impress these Lakota with our appearance, accoutrements, generosity and most of all purpose-driven discipline. I pray that one or more of the band may speak some French as English is generally unknown to these tribes. Conducting a parley in sign language would be taxing and underproductive. Whether Drouillard is capable of any eloquence in French remains to be determined.

Captain Meriwether Lewis.

The strong southwesterly flow diminishes throughout the day. The bright blue sky retreats from the advancing clouds to the west. By evening an overcast of clouds hangs over the prairie for as far as the eye can see. As day gives way to evening the overcast becomes darker, and darker – ominous. During the night the storm arrives. It is not a dangerous storm merely one of nuisance, creating a wet and, muddy camp. The men, having unpacked their dress uniforms, fail to repack these in their oilskin bags.

Freshly brushed, wool uniforms now look and smell like a herd of sodden sheep. Brass is already beginning to tarnish. The previous night's preparations are wasted on the day's weather.

It is decided not to proceed up the river and to the expected encounter with the Lakota this day. The river has come up slightly, but the sound of the not so far off falls has increased measurably.

Meriwether does not wish that at first meeting to look and smell like a pack of rats. The Lakota have lived here for centuries, they can wait to meet the delegation representing the United States of America one more day.

Two Tongues is a bit surprised that these whites should cower in their encampment like dogs. The Great Spirit has blessed the land with a life-giving gentle rain. The ponies will eat well, game will fatten, his band will thrive. In lieu of a parley, he will dance and sing praise to the Great Spirit.

Although the churning, counter-clockwise rotating storm has lifted and abated as it pushes toward the northeast, Lewis decides to rest and refit yet another day or two. He watches for the river to subside and return to its normal, late-summer flow and for the deafening roar of the cascades to quiet. He ponders just how long he can make the Lakota wait without causing irreparable irritation. He scratches an entry into his journal.

Waiting out a summer storm and anticipating meeting a Lakota party soon. In my experience, the Red Man is impatient after having taken a longer than necessary time to debate any given matter. I will make him wait a little longer in order to fluster any parley plan he may have. Even such a small tactical edge may prove helpful in what I expect to be a spirited meeting.

Meriwether Lewis.

As Lewis takes time to tactically plan his *parley,* Two Tongues and his party dance and sing.

Muffled words and a steady drum beat floats with the air. The drum beat, and the singing can not quite be discerned as makes it way toward the heavens, but the distant beat and occasional voice print are disconcerting to Lewis' men. Some of the men have distinct memories of Indian Wars in the East and Two Tongues praise and prayers serve only to make them nervous and fearful.

Finally, after four days of weather and waiting, the order is given to break camp and board the vessels. Today White Man will meet Red, an encounter will reverberate on the plains for decades to come.

Lewis takes up a gallant, Greek hero-like poise on the bow of the keelboat, Clark closer to the pilot house. The men, both in the keelboat and aboard the pirogues, are dressed in their best uniforms and conduct their duties stiffly as they know they are being watched.

Two Tongues sits astride his best pony dressed as the sub-chief he is; fine moccasins, elk hide leggings, a French-made cotton shirt, bone breastplate, his quill-braided hair stiff with oil. He applies no face or body paint. He will meet these whites as he is. The warriors accompanying him today are dressed similarly.

As the Corps of Discovery flotilla round a bend in the river, Two Tongues is visible to all, there on the western bank. Lewis orders a pirogue to come alongside the keelboat and boards.

Clark will remain with the keelboat, the hired civilians and all-important supplies at anchor in the river. One pirogue will proceed with Lewis, Seaman the dog, Douillard, eight uniformed men and the gifts. Nothing has been left to chance. The keelboat swivel gun is loaded with shot and primed, the second pirogue is tied up alongside to be used as a reinforcement or rescue boat as required. Tantalizingly, York is ordered to remain visible on deck. Ashore, only Lewis and Douillard are to speak.

Lewis' pirogue runs up on the muddy shore. Lewis is greeted by Two Tongues who raises his right arm, his left holding his lance and reins. Lewis too raises his right arm in greeting, jumps out of the pirogue together with Seaman and sloshes ashore. The boat is secured and the detail follows. Once assembled on shore, the detail stand in a semi-circle behind their commander as Lewis sets up and sits on a portable camp stool. Seaman sits next to his master, Douillard next to Seaman. Two Tongues raises his hand again and begins to speak in Lakota.

Notes: 62) La., *Tanyan yahipi* – Good Morning. 63) Fr., *Bon jour, mes freres. Bienvenue chez nous* – Good morning, my brothers. Welcome to OUR land.

Tanyan yahipi[62]. Says Two Tongues. Douillard without prompting replies, *Tanyan yahipi.* With this Lewis shoots Douillard a disapproving sideways glance indicating that he is not to speak, only interpret! Two Tongues then speaks again, *Bon jour, mes freres. Bienvenue chez nous*[63] Douillard slightly winces, Two Tongues implied meaning is quite clear.

"*Je m'appelle L'Homme De Deux Parole*[64]".

"He says that his name is Two Tongues, Cap't. And he welcomes you as brothers to HIS land." Interprets Douillard.

"Very well. I am Captain Meriwether Lewis, "Chief of a Corps of Discovery. I am sent here by the Great White Father."

Drouillard interprets Lewis' words and Lewis continues.

"As you are Lakota, we are Americans. Your land is the land of the Lakota, our land is the United States of America. We come in peace. We come as brothers. We come to talk, and smoke and learn. We will do these things, we will give you gifts and then we will move on, up the river to the Great Mountains and across to the sea. Tell us your story. Tell us about your people; how you live, how you pray and who you are? Then we will tell you about ourselves." Says Lewis.

Lewis then turns his head back toward his men and quietly orders that a pouch of tobacco be passed forward. With the tobacco pouch in hand, Lewis slowly stands up and offers Two Tongues the pouch laid across both hands outstretched. He bows slightly.

Two Tongues is inwardly impressed with this white man's manners but he maintains the "poker face" that his race is famous for. He accepts the proffered pouch and in turn calls for his pipe.

Note: 64) Fr., *Je m'appelle L'Homme De Deux Paroles.* I am Two Tongues

A few minutes pass. The pipe is filled and lit. Two Tongues places the soft stone stem of the pipe between his lips, closes his eyes and inhales. After a moment, he exhales and speaks.

"Good smoke"

Lewis also quietly exhales. The initial danger is past.

Two Tongues closes his eyes again, then speaks. He recites an oral history to Lewis, from deep down within his being. "There was another world before this one. But It was destroyed by the Great Spirit. The old world had become bad and ugly. That world was washed away in a great flood of water. Only a crow survived.

The crow needed a place to set down on dry land, so he pleaded with the Great Spirit to make yet another world where he could set down and place his feet. The Great Spirit heard the crow's pleas and separated the waters, and dry land appeared. The crow was grateful. The next day the crow asked the Great Spirit if it would not repopulate world some? The Great Spirit reached down into the mud and pulled out an otter, then a beaver, and a turtle. It created other animals and birds also, placing these in a Sacred Pipe Pouch. Later, men and women were made from red, yellow and white clay. This is the beginning of our world.

My father's, father's, fathers have dwelled here upon this land since then. We follow the seasons and tatanka[65] from these rivers where the sun rises, to the Great Mountains, where the sun reposes. In summer, we move our lodges north toward the Land of the Crow. In winter, we move our lodges south, toward the Land of the Kiowa. We follow *tatanka*, who through the Great Spirit feeds, clothes and shelters my people, the Lakota. We dance, sing and praise the Great Spirit who created, guides and keeps his people. This is who we are."

Note: 65) La., *tatanka* — buffalo

Lewis is somewhat taken back by the similarities of Two Tongues history to the Hebrew stories in Genisis. Lewis says nothing however. He pauses, then speaks. "We too were created by God, The Great Spirit, in his image. We were created in a land far away which was also destroyed in a great flood because it had become bad and ugly. God spared a few men and women and pairs of animals and birds. With these, by his Grace, he repopulated the earth. Therefore, we too are your brothers."

Both leaders, The Red and the White are surprised at themselves, and the unexpected direction of this *parley*. So unnerved by Two Tongues recitation of the Lakata story of creation, Lewis calls to end the *parley*. Lewis proposes that they meet again on the morrow to discuss other things, and what they as men and leaders can do. Privately, he wishes to consult with Clark and see just how a peer and trusted acquaintance reacts to what he has just heard.

Both chiefs, Two Tongues and Lewis step back to the comfort of their worlds and the sanctity of their own thoughts.

That evening Lewis and his co-commander discuss the strange *parley* with Two Tongues. Clark, more conventional than Lewis, seems less disturbed that the Lakota would identify their history beginning after a great flood and that the Great Spirit would make man from clay. Lewis, on the other hand, is greatly disturbed. Lewis the scarcher of the Northwest Passage, Lewis the seeker of the hairy pachyderm and enigmatic ape-man sees his views of his faith and purpose turned upside down. He pens a note in his journal.

Today we sat with the Lakota. I exchanged words, held a parley with a sub-chief named Two Tongues. He told me that his people with created from clay by God. He told me that his God had destroyed this world by flood, due to its evil. I wonder if it isn't the itinerant Jesuits who roamed this region in the 17th century, the Papists who somehow inserted or overlay the Hebrew into the indigenous oral histories. This would explain many things but not everything. I am less convinced today that these aborigines are heathen or somehow less than us. Those that have not yet been polluted by the White Man seem to me to be more like long-lost brothers than untamed savages.

Lewis senses *déjà vu* as he boards the pirogue for the *parley*. It is hot. It is windy. Even the river is rough and covered in whitecaps. The river looks more like shallow, churned-up Chesapeake Bay in a nordeaster, than the Mighty Missouri River in fall. Already, only halfway to the parley encampment, Lewis and the others are sweating through their army-issue, woolen, blue uniforms. Lewis orders, "Remove and stow your jackets!" A jacketless detachment in blue trousers, boots and bleached white, cotton shirts look so much better than sweat-sodden, smelly uniform jackets.

Speaking to himself, Lewis mumbles. "Were it not for the expense, cotton fabric should be used for summer dress uniforms. These wool tunics are acceptable to the Yankee in spring and fall, but something lighter will be required for an army on these plains."

At the Lakota camp Lewis again tries to seize the initiative. Lewis attempts the tried and true "Great White Father to his children" speech. On a more docile band, on a less seasoned sub-chief, on a cooler day, Lewis' speech may have been heard out, but Two Tongues is in no mood to humor the young commander. Two Tongues speaks.

"We have heard the words of Sub-Chief Lewis. We pay our respects to the Great White Father, Lewis' Chief. We Lakota respect our enemies and pay homage only to the Great Spirit. Our peoples however are tied together by The Great Spirit. We, therefore, are brothers. In the spirit of brotherhood, we will accept your gifts and allow you to continue across and away from Lakota land. We will smoke to your successful journey. We will dance and sing in praise of It's creation. Now go in peace."

Lewis understands that Two Tongues will not be easily seduced, especially by the theoretical omnipotence of the Great White Father. Trade, a show of strength perhaps, or a mutually beneficial treaty might be ways to deal with these Lakota. But what do the Lakota covet of the White man? Very little indeed! They pride themselves as warriors, they admire a swift horse or a nice remuda, they follow *tatanka*. There seems to be no easy answers as to how to appeal to, or, of course, subjugate, then integrate the Lakota into an Industrial Age and American society.

Two Tongues also mentally gathers his collective experiences with the Whites. While it is true that trade goods such as ironware, cloth and weapons are desirable, these may come at too heavy of price for his people. True, the Pawnee fall more easily from a rifle ball than from an arrow, but what of a warrior's pride? Where is the honor in killing one's enemy before you can see his face? A warrior needs to see the fear in his enemy's eyes, to smell his breath and experience his foe pierced by the lance and falling limp upon it. This is the way of the Lakota warrior. But the Whites are on a collision course with the world of the Lakota. Two Tongues can sense this. He may have dismissed Lewis and his men with ease, but more Whites are sure to follow. The Lakota must adapt to survive. How to adapt, what to adopt, these are questions for someone with more medicine than Two Tongues. These are questions however that need to be addressed during Two Tongue's lifetime, not later. Two Tongues and his brothers must act to save their children and their grandchildren from the Whites.

Chapter 13

TO PARTS UNKNOWN

In the morning, after two days of *parley* with Two Tongues and his Lakota, a week in camp on the eastern shore of the Missouri just south of the falls, the expedition is again underway and again Lewis holds a long, thoughtful conversation with himself.

A strong southwesterly flow greets us this morning. It is good to feel the wind in the cool of the morning, but we will pay the price for it this afternoon when this cooling breeze becomes a hot, dry, desiccating wind. The keelboat men seem happy, having set a sail and running with the wind. Today they will not pole nor pull the barge in a long line of them tethered each to a rope, slogging along in the shallows. Even the pirougues have set their small sails and are enjoying the ride.

I am happy to distance ourselves from Two Tongues and his band of Lakota. I will continue to set a strong watch should Two Tongues become tempted to try to take from us the chest of gifts and other goods. In spite of his savage innocence, I cannot trust him. A pig is a pig, a dog is a dog and an Indian is an Indian. His very culture encourages theft, and should we challenge such a theft, well then, tragedy would likely follow. Our pickets should dissuade him from such a temptation. Seaman aids us in this task. It is hard not to draw his notice.

The panoramic depth and breadth of the land are awe inspiring. Each day, Douillard and, now Corporal Bratton set out early, maintaining a mile or so distance from the main body.

Game has become scarcer, but snakes more plentiful. Consequently, Bratton and Douillard have changed tactics. The brittle snapping of twigs and grasses announce the arrival of the hunter/scouts and resident rattlesnakes guard their territories with a warning of the rattle.

Antelope, deer, even rabbits know the sound and change course. Bratton and Douillard only slow the pace, even stopping to identify the predator become prey.

Corporal Bratton has adapted to the change. Instead of carrying his musket at the ready, or loading it with shot instead of ball, he has constructed an odd, bayonet like device on its end.

The four-pronged, stout, wooden attachment is made to grab and hold the head of a snake.

Once held, Bratton can cut off the snake's head without fear of being bitten or his prey escaping. Simple, but exceeding clever, Bratton's Switch, as the men have named it, has put many a snake in the stew.

The men are becoming used to eating Bratton's fare of snake. Roasted, the white meat is sinewy and full of tiny bones. Stewed however the snake meat is good. The French keelboat men, fond of Great Lakes Whitefish, smoked or boiled, have taken up calling Bratton's fare, the Whitefish of the desert. Lewis is pleased at how both the men, cooks and hunters have adapted to their environment. Even more adapting is certain to be required before this adventure is at an end.

"What's on the plate tonight?" Lewis asking joking, already knowing the answer.

"Bratton's fare, sir" Replies a cook.

"Stewed or stewed" Asks Lewis.

"Stewed, sir" Replies the cook with a smile.

On occasion, Seaman, Lewis' Newfoundland accompanies either Douillard or Bratton into the bush. The noisy rummagings of the dog-beast are infinitely less concerning now that big game hunting has become snaking and the local Lakota band, spoken for by Two Tongues, has granted Lewis' expedition free passage north and out of Sioux territory.

At a distance, and in a stealthy manner, Two Tongues continues to parallel the river and the Corps of Discovery, just to the west. Two Tongues is determined to relieve Lewis of Seaman, the magnificent Newfoundland, and Corps' mascot. Just how he will accomplish this napping of the dog-beast without harm or killings is still a question in his mind. Had he not asked the white leader to give or trade him the dog? Had he not been honorable and forthright in his desire to acquire the beast? Two Tongues cannot understand the ways of these whites. He met them, he greeted them as brothers, he smoked with them and fed them. True, the whites did offer some gifts, but not at all what he clearly desired. Still, he granted the whites safe passage through Lakota territory, all in good faith. But now, Two Tongues must act as would any true Lakota warrior, he will take that which he desires by daring and stealth and count coup upon his enemy. Two Tongues will take back his pride, damaged in treating with these whites.

It is cooler today and Seaman rushes through the brush seeking scents that only a dog would know. He is about 100 yards ahead of Bratton and a mile or more distant from the keelboat and pirogues on the river. Suddenly the dog takes to the scent of fresh meat, not cooked meats, not the scraps which he is accustomed to, but fresh, blood oozing meat. Within moments he locates and claim his prize – a rabbit haunch. To his surprise, another scent then a man appears, a man he has smelled and seen just a day or two before, Two Tongues the Lakota, the man with whom his master smoked, ate and parleyed. Seaman is not alarmed by the somewhat familiar red man and is collared with a rawhide lash and is being led away as Bratton stumbles upon the dog-napping. Two Tongues has taken just a moment or two longer than he had planned and by doing so, has brought ruin to his scheme of daring and stealth. He has been found out, but refuses to change course.

"Let go of that dog!" Demands Bratton lowering his rifle to Two Tongues belly. Two Tongues does not speak, rather turns his back to Bratton and attempts to walk away. Seaman resists giving Bratton time to prime his weapon and order the dog's release again.

"Get your thieving red paws off of that dog!" Threatens Bratton once again. This time, Bratton locks his loaded weapon into the firing position, places his finger on the trigger and aims at the back of Two Tongue's chest. The distinctive "click" of Bratton locking his weapon is a sound even Two Tongues cannot ignore. A warrior cannot suffer death in showing his heel.

Two Tongues turns and confronts Bratton. He unsheathes his knife but does not step toward the young hunter/scout.

Douillard has somehow picked-up Bratton's threatening voice in the wind, and has quickly found his way to his side. He whispers out loud to his hunter/scout partner. "Back off a pace or two and you'll be less likely to lose your manhood. These Redsticks are handy with a knife. He might lose face by killing you, but he'd be happy to turn you into a steer." States Douillard as a matter of fact.

As Bratton steps back, Drouillard steps forward, rifle held low in a carrying position and right hand extended for the lash. Two Tongues has been offered a way out of his dilemma. He does not relinquish his prize to the threats of the young man, rather releases the lash and allows the dog to return to the older, non-threatening half-white, Douillard.

In spite of failing to steal Seaman, Two Tongues turns his pony and nudges her flanks. He and his party will move south by southwest, back toward his people, Old Smoke Chief and their encampment. He brings with him a few odd trinkets proffered by Lewis including Jefferson's silver medal of peace and brotherhood. For a moment he ponders the lofty ideal of peace and brotherhood between his people, and these whites. The thought dissipates in his mind as quickly as Lewis' little fleet disappear up the river.

Douillard removes the rawhide lash from Seaman. He runs free. Bratton, manhood intact, breathes a sign of relief. The Lakota have disappeared onto the plain.

Upon receiving Douillard and Bratton's reports, Lewis continues to write in his own journal.

After several days, we have finally freed ourselves from the Lakota. These Lakota seem to be the most aggressive of the bands we have encountered so far. They are well mounted and territorial. I suspect we, and others who follow, will have difficulties in negotiating terms with them. I liken them somewhat to the Shawnee and Mingo of the Ohio Valley who have and continue to resist American interests west of the Appalachians.

This great Missouri River leads us north by northwest. It is a great fishery but the men desire meat. Game has become somewhat scarce. Snakes and hares have provided adequate and tasty fare these past several weeks but as the cold has descended upon us, the snakes have withdrawn to their dens and the hares have become skittish being the prime target of every meat-eating creature in God's creation. We have still some flour, salt, molasses, parched corn and whiskey but the bacon, beans and others staples and essentials are exhausted. As I predicted, we are underfunded and short of supplies for such an ambitious expedition. The aboriginals are unimpressed with our gifts.

The land along the Missouri is brown and dry, but fair weather has eased the journey's burden. On the horizon, a diagonal line appears foretelling change and soon.

Lewis continues undeterred by weather not yet revealed, but continually scans the western sky, as he notes the falling barometer readings. The storm front approaches. Too late Lewis finally orders the boats ashore and shelters prepared – the first squall line is only miles away.

The clouds of the squall are so low that it seems one could touch them, as the green-hued waves roll overhead. The men feverishly pitch their tents. A grey, hissing wall of rain follows the wave a half a mile or so behind. A sheet of cold, wind-driven rain descends upon all. It will be a miserable night.

Careful not to expose his journal to the elements, Lewis writes.

A cold, hard rain has engulfed us. Both temperature and barometric pressure have dropped precipitously. I sense snow is not far off. I hope that I am in error.

Gradually the winds abate. The sheets of rain continue their march to the east but have left the camp sodden and muddy. The gloomy low clouds have given away to a broken, hopeful sky but the winds increase again and the temperature drops more than forty degrees. More clouds on the horizon, as snow makes it first appearance on the fall prairie.

The next days and weeks become increasingly difficult for the Corps. Leaden skies generate snow showers, some afternoons tease with a hint of sun. But it is the wind, ceaseless from the north and northwest, following the Missouri River valley like a conduit to somewhere undefined. These winds are increasingly strong, without buffer on the open plain. Douillard and Bratton find even the ubiquitous ratters have taken to their dens leaving only mice and increasingly few hares as seasonal prey for all predators; coyote, hawk, eagle and man. Lewis' hunters produce less as the men devour the remaining stores. The men, working hard against the cold current and relentless winds burn energy at an astonishing rate. They require more food.

"Cap't, the boys can't survive on rabbit stew and johnny cakes, especially given there's so few rabbits. The johnny cakes fluff-up the belly for a while, but even then there are only a few barrels of flour remaining.

Batton can scout ahead and take what small game can be found. I'll move off to the west hopefully not raising the hackles of the Lakota. Perhaps I can flush-out an Elk or Buffalo. I may be gone a day or two." States Drouillard in a manner seeking approval.

"I believe that you have a good plan there, Drouillard. Take no more than seven days out and back. You'll be able to locate us by our campsites along the river. Good luck, Godspeed."

Affirms Lewis.

Chapter 14

DROUILLARD

The big Frenchman requires little and takes less as he departs the Missouri River valley and moves west toward, what he hopes will be better hunting grounds. The long-haired, thickly-bearded man blends well in his heavy buffalo coat, knee-high boots and natural wool tuck. He carries powder, ball, a tin of charcoal cloth tinder, flint, steel, some parched corn and a wooden canteen of whiskey. He recons that he can find water anywhere on the dry landscape, whiskey is a rarer commodity on the plains. He completes his outfit with a .66 caliber rifle and knife. On the open prairie, he requires no compass.

Drouillard walks at a steady, measured pace, he misses nothing. A broken twig, a scuffed stone, grass once laid upon, scat, they all tell a story and ultimately lead to a game trail. He follows his senses and intuitions and after only a half day, he comes upon a brace of antelope in a break. The loud report of the .66 caliber, big bore gun breaks the silence of the plains.

Drouillard is pleased, an antelope at last! At least initially, his stratagem has proven correct. He decides to return to the Corps this very day, carrying with him his fresh kill.

First the animal is dressed, removing the head, entrails and lower limbs. He lunches on the antelope's liver. Next Drouillard fashions a light travois of willow branches upon which he places his kill and which he will pull back to the Missouri. Resting now, he is pleased that the sun indicates no more than half the day has passed.

After a short lunch of roasted antelope liver, washed down with some water from the spring and chased with a shot of whiskey, Drouillard lifts the buggy-shaft like travois poles and strains forward as it begins to slide. At a steady pace, the little travois slides across the prairie. The big man never waivers, step after step, mile upon mile, even as his trunk-like legs begin to tingle and burn. After only a short afternoon, he sights the river valley, then picks up his pace to an overlook where he hopes to spot the strange, little flotillas making its way up river.

It is fully dark when Monsieur Drouillard pulls his antelope-laden travois into camp, even as he is stopped by the sentry.

"Who goes there?" Challenges the picket as he lowers his weapon.

"C'est moi, tu idiot! C'est Drouillard avec la cuisine." Replies Drouillard unimpressed with the half-hearted challenge.

Buoyed by Drouillard's successful hunt, the men let out a great cheer. "Huzzah!"

As morning dawns, both Drouillard and Bratton prepare for their respective hunts; Drouillard to the west, Bratton just ahead and along the river. Drouillard raises his mighty paw and waves as he sets out again to the west in search of game. Bratton waves and continues north by northwest following the west bank of the river.

Unlike his first, lucky day, Drouillard is unable to jump a deer, elk or antelope on this first day out. He has seen no buffalo sign at all. The second day, produces a similar result., only tantalizing tracks and scat indicating the presence of game. That night, not fearing to attract local aborigines, Drouillard makes a generous campfire, eats a little jerky and parched corn chased by a generous portion of whiskey. He wraps himself tightly in his buffalo robe coat, mumbles a little song and drifts off to sleep next to the fire.

Drouillard's sense of smell is the first to alert him, even in his sleep. Only when he feels himself rolled over like a log in his buffalo robe coat does he open one sleep-crusted eye. His vision clears quickly however as a large, black-brown snout comes into focus. The Grizzly sniffs its find. Drouillard is unable to free himself from the confines of his coat as the bear rolls him again, looking a soft underbelly in order to sample this strange animal. Drouillard struggles to free himself from the huge omnivore.

Wiggling like an armless, legless invertebrate, Drouillard moves just enough in order to cock back his right, stump-like leg and kick with all his power into the curious snout of the bear. The bear lets go angry roar as it rises up onto his haunches. Thinking quickly, Drouillard leaps up, grabbing neither rifle nor knife, but a stout branch still smoldering in the fire. Sweeping the branch in a crisscross motion and bringing the flame back to life, Drouillard now possesses the only thing that might frighten a bear – flame. Moving forward into the attack, he thrusts the burning branch into the nose of the bear, singeing the fur of its snout. It roars again, but takes one step back. Drouillard swings the flaming branch again. The bear drops to all fours, growls again, then turns away. Both bear and man will live another day.

"Well, all be God-damned and go to hell, I need a drink." Curses Drouillard.

Note: 66) Fr. *C'est moi, tu idiot! C'est Drouillard avec la cuisine.* It's me, you idiot. It's Drouillard with supper.

Chapter 15

A CURIOSITY IN THE SAND

Every day more miles, miles into a largely unknown, unmapped and undefined wilderness. Often boredom plagues both men and officers, alike. The men row, or pole or pull, slowly but steadily dragging the little fleet, against the current, now icy cold, up the river. Lewis and Clark, read, write and record. Daydreaming, and thinking about the ancient and undiscovered, Lewis notices something out of sorts embedded in the sandstone wall of the embankment. He retrieves his leather-cased spyglass and peers closely. He discerns the object, but sees only an odd, shiny reflection against the weakening afternoon light.

"We'll put in and set up camp on that gravel bar along the embankment. It is late enough and there is something I wish to investigate in the morning." Orders Lewis.

A routine camp is made and the men count their lucky stars for the extra hour or so to tend personal needs or just relax. Morale tonight is better than usual.

Lewis is up early the next morning, out of habit but in excited anticipation of discovering exactly what he could have seen embedded in the sandstone embankment. He walks over to the cliff-like wall of the embankment but can not quite reach the object, if it is an object. He returns to camp for a ladder, pick, and shovel.

One or two of the men would be of great assistance, I will detail them. He says to himself.

"Sergeant Ordway!" Calls Lewis. Ordway appears before Lewis after only a minute or two.

"Sergeant, assemble a short detail of three men. Have them bring a ladder, a shovel and a pick. A non-com is not necessary. I will command. This is a sort of personal excursion." Explains Lewis.

"Aye, sir. A short detail of three diggers. I've got just the men in mind." Replies Ordway a bit too quickly.

"No, no Ordway. This is not a fatigue detail. No punishment intended. This may be delicate.

Make certain that I have good and careful men. Assemble in 10 minutes." Counters Lewis.

"Yes, sir. 10 minutes, sir." Confirms Ordway Lewis and his detail return to the site. Fortunately, the ladder, steadied by strong hands is sufficient to reach the object. Once Lewis views the object close up. He is disappointed. It, at first, appears to be nothing more than a large Buffalo skull, but then again not. The more Lewis probes and digs around the object, he realizes that it is; larger than buffalo skull, strong like bone, yet more fragile. Obviously, it is not the remains of an ape man or a pachyderm, but something else. Lewis continues his dig. The more he digs into the crumbling sandstone, the object begins to reveal itself. He thinks back on reading George Cuvier's, *L'histoire naturelle des animaux,* An Elementary Survey of the Natural History of Animals, and his "correlation of parts." Regardless of today's outcome, this is the first bit of personal fun he has experienced during this month's long expedition.

The men back in camp "stand down". Lewis continues to dig, oblivious of time. By day's end, he has, somewhat unscientifically excavated the skull of a creature totally unknown to him. The shape of the object is not unlike that of a lizard. The jaw and snout are large with many oversized, serrated incisors remaining. The, yet to be cleaned eye sockets are huge. It appears to be bone but crumbles easily. Much to his dismay, Lewis has already lost a piece or two.

With considerable effort, the excavated object is gently passed down the ladder and placed on a blanket, where the detail men gather around and stare.

"We'll place the object aboard the keelboat where I can work on it. I'm not sure what we have here boys, but it is something not many men have seen. Back to camp and be careful of today's find." Says Lewis.

Lewis had intended to place object aboard the keelboat where he could work on it at his leisure. Once it was aboard however, fascinated by his find, he does not order camp to be broken and the continuation of the journey upriver. Lewis spends the next few days chiseling, cleaning and examining what appears to be the fossilized remains of a giant lizard cranium, a skull of an obviously carnivorous creature. In spite of dropping temperatures, and Clark's urging, the Corps of Discovery remains at the "discovery" site.

"I know that you want me to continue up river, William, but this discovery is the *raison d'etre* of our expedition here and we have discovered something more than a new species of fish or a ground squirrel. What we have discovered here pre-dates humanity and certainly throws into question the traditional Judeo-Christian timeline of natural history. Obviously, these creatures roamed the earth before man. Therefore, the commonly accepted biblical timeline of creation; Adam to Noah, Noah to Abraham, Abraham to David and David to us does not work. I was seeking legends, legends of giant ape-like men or hairy pachyderms, not something pre-historic like this.

The Missouri waters have washed away a millennia of sandstone encasing this object. I am afraid if I leave the site, spring floods may erase any further evidence of this find. Let's linger here a day or two more and see if we can uncover any further objects." Explains Lewis.

"You are the in command, Meriwether. I understand your point, but the bigger picture is that we need to find a suitable place for winter camp or our Corps of Discovery may very well become fossils ourselves." Chides Clark.

Remaining at the site, much to Lewis' disappointment, only a few additional relics are discovered. A vertebrate and one other additional, but unidentifiable fossils are sifted from the soil, stone and debris. It is time to move on. Lewis finishes up the dig, and orders the expedition to continue.

An hour or so before poling away from shore, Drouillard comes into sight, dragging the little *travois* behind him. He has had to backtrack many miles south, having assumed the expedition would have made better forward progress these past few days, oblivious to the pause at the dig. Clark welcomes Drouillard.

"Good to see you again, Drouillard. I see that your topknot is still firmly in place." Jokes Clark.

"*Oui, mon Capitain*, every hair precisely where it has been placed by God. No Indians but some sign here and there. Unfortunately, I saw little game as well, though I did manage a venison or two. Why are you not farther up river. I have come back south more than ten miles, I think? Reports Douillard.

"True. We have been delayed here for nearly a week. Captain Lewis discovered some interesting bones and ordered us to remain. We are now preparing to resume the expedition." Explains Clark, somewhat revealing his disagreement.

"Ah." Drouillard says no more.

By mid-day the little fleet is once again progressing slowly up the river. The men are rested, and have lunched on smoked venison, compliments of the big French hunter. The weather is mild today and Lewis sits on the deck of the keelboat and pens in his journal.

November 4, 1804

We spent the better part of the week excavating an object embedded in sandstone in an outcropping some days north of the Falls. Upon its successful excavation, cleaning and examination, I have determined the object to be a fossilized remain of a great beast, a reptilian carnivore predating human history.

It is not a secret to my President or to my men that I have a passion for mystery. Since my childhood, I have heard indigenous tales of the fantastic, giant ape-like men, seldom seen but universally feared, and great hairy pachyderms with protruding tusks reaching the ground. These elephant-like beasts were once hunted by aboriginal ancestors as commonly as buffalo are hunted today. I have even touched relics said to have been carved from their great ivory tusks. For me to have discovered an object unknown and outside of even indigenous tales, is, well, a dream beyond measure. But, as with most things of the fantastic, it is a sword with two edges. First, The Find. A new mystery, further and future investigation and hypothesis. Second, The Challenge. The very existence of the object, its beginnings and end, bring into question all that which has been so carefully documented in the Genesis of Judeo-Christian beliefs. Where does my carnivorous lizard fit among the creatures so carefully created by God the Father? Are the Garden, the clay-formed Adam, his rib-begotten wife Eve, the lion and the lamb merely shepherd tales of creation? Was the earth not created by God out of the void in just six days? If this object throws Genesis into question, then not also Exodus, Kings, Judges and the rest? Are our sacred Gospels safe from discreated Testaments of Old? These questions weigh heavily on me. I am sleepless, yet curious and inquiring as to the object and frightened as to what the object's mere existence in the nascent struggle between Church and natural history. Then again, why should religious teachings be at odds with science? If God did create the heavens and the earth, should this not be reflected and evident in earth science? I find there are more questions than answers.

I will discern on these questions as time permits. As for the Corps, we will continue north by northwest or as the river guides us for only a week or two more.

Game is scarce, the weather degrades and we must construct a defensible yet habitable fort soon. We require wood for both construction and warmth, well-drained and safe from spring waters. I very much doubt we will find an abundance of game, but friendly bands with whom trade is possible would be the best possible scenario.

Meriwether Lewis

Chapter 16

INTO WINTER QUARTERS

46 degrees, 5 minutes, 6 seconds north, 100 degrees, 37 minutes, 49 seconds west. Sunrise at 0703, sunset at 1657. Temperature 33 degrees. Barometric pressure 29.98 inches of mercury. Leaden skies, a wind from the northwest. Notes Lewis in his journal.

Since entering the mouth of the Missouri River, Lieutenant William Clark has dutifully used position, compass, and alidade, turning mathematical calculations into detailed, hand-drawn maps of the river valley, annotated with scraps of information added by Bratton & Drouillard.

The resultant twelve pages accurately depicts the little fleet's journey up the river, so far as the Corps has advanced. Together with Lewis' positional and other data, an accurate set of maps and almanac begin to form. In the beginning, the only reliable source of such information was the so-called "beaver map" published by Herman Moll in 1715. Moll was reputedly not the primary source however, his information, for the most part, conveniently lifted from a French map of some decades before. Linear distances have been stepped off, measured with a perambulator or just guessed at. Surprisingly, combined with all the data collected, a fairly accurate measurement.

To the west, Drouillard continues the hunt, roughly paralleling the river 7-10 miles out. Bratton and Seaman reconnoiter and jump shoot a mile or so ahead of the flotilla. The men move the little fleet, while their officers calculate, observe and journal the expedition. Each day they forge on into the coming winter and each day Lewis is closer to declaring winter camp. A certain nervousness pervades the company, a company anxious to prepare as best they can for a cold, dark winter which is surely on the horizon. In spite of a general anxiety, the pace quickens in anticipation of winter camp and settling in. The men can imagine winter hardships, but also, they look forward to more leisurely days when keeping warm, eating and maintaining equipment are the only Orders of the Day. The possibilities of the round buttocks and soft bellies of a willing squaw also illuminate their imaginations.

The gathering, preserving and cataloging of mineral, flora & fauna is a task requiring patience, attention to detail and time. It would seem that Meriwether and William have an abundance of time, but quite the opposite seems to be true. Meriwether spends many a day sorting, storing and cataloging the collections. William spends his time on logistical matters and his map. It is a good and balanced division of labor and they get along with one another well. Deferred is the conversation about York and the Rights of Man. Perhaps this will take place while in winter camp?

"I intend to catalog and package all these samples for the return voyage of the keelboat in the spring. I intend to include even the prairie dog pet we've acquired. God willing all these items will be headed down river come April. Hopefully our cashe will reach the President by early summer. After breaking winter camp, we will continue to follow the Missouri to wherever she will take us. We will require more canoes for cargo and the men. We can fashion these native-style from the cottonwoods over the winter months.

Every morning Meriwether first; checks, then winds his pocket watch, he then checks the temperature, and barometric readings, he observes sunrise, wind direction, and sky then logs these observations. This ritual has become a ritual akin to *matins*, morning prayer.

William supervises reveille, then checks the expedition's stores. He samples breakfast and gauges the morale of the men. This too has become a ritual, the difference being he softly utters morning prayers. 46 degrees, 14 minutes, 58 seconds north, 100 degrees, 38 minutes, 19 seconds west. How much farther will the river run north? At some point it must turn to the west toward the Great Mountains and the Pacific Ocean? How much farther?

Mornings are increasingly cold, afternoons more tolerable, but the celestial signs are clear that winter is fast approaching. The Corps of Discovery has, in recent days, past and noted two smaller tributaries of the great river. These were not explored as they, most probably, would not materially contribute to the mission. But each these rivlets show sign of human activity, no doubt the Mandan and Hidatsa, well documented by French hunters and trappers, are nearby.

At 47 degrees, 17 minutes, 27 seconds north, 101 degrees, 17 minutes, 6 seconds west the great Missouri turns sharply west by northwest. The eastern bank of the river is higher here, carved-out by eons of spring waters. Cottonwood grow thickly, and deadfall lays aplenty. Meriwether halts the year's campaign.

In an unusual afternoon assembly Capt. Meriwether Lewis speaks to the men.

"In this year, 1804, much has been asked of you by your nation, President, Lieutenant Clark and myself and without doubt, to some degree, of yourselves. We have arrived at this great westward turn in the river just as winter begins to descend upon us. Here we will erect a fortified camp, on these bluffs, and endeavor to further prepare ourselves for the barren, cold months ahead. Come spring, the Corps will continue in its quest for the Northwest Passage and the sea. The keelboat and hired men will return to St. Louis with our collections, samples, mail and reports.

Lieutenant Clark, Order of the Day – build warm huts, an administration lodge protected by a palisade at least 8 feet tall. There is to be one stout gate and a sally port. That is all for today, men. We begin our labors tomorrow."

The Mandan and Hidatsa, near the confluence of the Missouri and two small, northeast flowing rivlets, in the area north of the falls where Lewis treated with the Lakota, are the Siouan-speaking Mandan and Hidatsa people. There are as many as 15,000 of these people in numerous villages, scattered along the cottonwood and scrub banks of the rivers. They precariously exist here on, an otherwise, barren prairie. Unlike their Lakota brethren, the Mandan and Hidatsa have a settled, agrarian lives. Their large, round, earthen lodges protect them from the harsh elements. These people trade both to the north and to the south, along the Missouri River.

Mandan and Hidatsa acquaintance with white men is first with French-Canadian traders moving up and down the river. Through these infrequent occurrences, the people have acquired coveted guns, steel knives, pots and cloth. From the Comanche and Lakota a few horses too have found their way into Mandan lives.

December 5, 1804

These past two mornings, early, 0300, I have witnessed for the first time the magnificence of the Aurora Borealis, so-called Northern Lights. Iridescent, green fingers of light dance on the northern horizon, changing shape every few minutes. The bases appear like a fog, almost purple in color. Numerous fingers protrude out of the base fog clawing at the starry sky. The Romans named this phenomena Aurora after the goddess of the dawn, Galileo believed this to be merely sunlight reflecting off of the earth, yet in Italian folklore these lights are a harbinger of bad tidings. Scientifically, our temperatures, barometric pressure and winds are unchanged. There is no noise associated with the lights. I dismiss the lights as an omen, but will

The Mandan and the Hidatsa are, semi-nomadic occupying five major villages in and around the westward bend of the Missouri River. These people have had some contact with white men, trading when an advantage might be gained, watching and discussing the passing of mostly French trappers toward the great mountains in the west.

Surprisingly, one of these wandering trappers is allowed to live amongst them, a Frenchman from the east who has cleverly traded for a young Shoshoni captive. He has taken, the barely pubescent teen as his wife and who is now heavily pregnant with his child. The man, Touissant Charbonnaeu is a rather useless human being who survives this world by his quick observations and his tongue.

The physical center of village life is the effigy of the "Lone Man", a painted, red cedar post representing the creator god, survivor of the great flood. For several days now, Lewis has desired to call on his indigenous neighbors out of courtesy and, of course, for essential information and trade but also pressingly to consult their holy man as to his interpretation of the Aurora these past two nights. A decision is made. Lewis dresses formally, his best uniform, brass and bears gifts.

In spite of their knowledge of and trade with the whites, some Hidatsa are openly hostile to the presence of these fifty or so white men wintering on their land, so near to their villages.

Buffalo Mane, their peace chief, calms the young warriors as best as he can, but he cannot dismiss their concerns and fears. Fortunately for Lewis and the Corps of Discovery, the Hidatsa village holy man, Knows All and Buffalo Mane receive Lewis with curiosity and hospitality. He is offered some dried berries, smoked fish and tobacco. Again, and as usual, after the "Great White Father" greeting, gifts are distributed and some small talk begins. Lewis is careful to always defer to Buffalo Mane, but it is to Knows All that his real questions are directed.

Warm, gathered around a fire in Buffalo Mane's lodge, Lewis queries Knows All about the Aurora phenomena. Knows All replies. "The Lone Man" speaks to his original people in many ways. We have but to listen. But man, even we, his original people, are too consumed in our own prowess and women in their gossip to listen to him as he speaks. Our ancestors, sometimes, speak also, with him, in him and through him. These lights of which you speak are but reflections of our people dancing before him, dancing the *"okipa"*, the sun dance, celebrating survival of the great flood and singing in the heavens. We welcome you in the peace of The Lone One."

It has been an eventful day for Captain Lewis, a day of possibilities but also of danger. Had the Hidatsa been hostile to the presence of fifty white men occupying Hidatsa land and constructing a fort even a temporary one, then either by neglect, winter or battle, it would be the end of The Corps of Discovery. The Aurora unknowingly created an opportunity for Lewis to intercourse with his new neighbors and to do so successfully. Lewis writes.

December 6, 1804

Today I departed camp and construction to investigate our indigenous neighbors, in this region both the Mandan and Hidatsa. As Providence may will it, the Hidatsa peace chief, Buffalo Mane, was curious about our party whereas their holy man, Knows All, shared my observations and interest in the Aurora. I made the usual but abbreviated speech — on behalf of our President and nation — and made a distribution of gifts. Thereafter, we shared information, the foundation of trust and trade. I learned of the Hidatsa interpretation of the Aurora, made the acquaintance of a possible interpreter/guide for the lands to the west and in the great mountains. I now better understand our own prospects here in the northern plains this winter. I have yet to show our neighbors the large lizard skull which I have had excavated

Lt. William Clark expertly supervises the construction of stout cabins, an administration structure as well as a palisade around the perimeter, a perhaps unnecessary but prudent, military precaution. The local aborigines seem to be willing and peaceful enough, but not all are pleased with the presence of the white men and a future trade, gaming or carnal misunderstanding could, potentially, lead to an altercation between one, two or more of each group. Some physical barricade may provide a degree of protection and separation until negotiations can settle the matter(s) satisfactorily. The only proper building materials for the lieutenant's construction project are the large cottonwood trees which populate the river bank environs. Cottonwoods are large trees, but soft and prone to insects and decay.

As Clark plans and the men measure and build, Lewis himself discerns and contemplates. He enters a metamorphosis of the mind whereby he begins to transcend the present, measures the accepted understanding of the past and ponders the future as well as his part in it. All of this brings him no peace, rather unsettles an already fragile balance in his mind.

"I must treat with that holy man again", he mumbles to himself. "The natives hint of a parallel world not unlike our own earthly and celestial but theirs is less adorned, more accessible. I must understand more".

The schooled and disciplined Captain Meriwether Lewis, U.S. Army is hardly a candidate to "go native" but something about Knows All acceptance of the unknown and mysteries of life robs Lewis' mind of what little peace it has.

"How can these natives talk about God the Creator, an apocalyptical flood and undying souls without ever having read the bible? What personal and tribal experiences have so grounded their understandings? I must learn more, yet communication is difficult and incomplete."

It is expected that there will be fewer opportunities for trade west of the Mandan villages.

The scattered, nomadic and wilder tribes to the west have had little intercourse with whites and should be generally avoided. Accordingly, more goods find there way into Mandan and Hidatsa hands due in part to this reason and the overriding concern about surviving the winter months. Goods for future trading will not benefit dead white men.

At an unofficial level, trading is already taking place between the men and the Hidatsa. A necklace, some powder & shot, a manufactured knife, even a comb will buy a tuss with a Hidatsa wife offered up by her husband. A roasted joint of venison, a few moments of bliss with a warm and surprisingly willing native woman – barter is barter.

Lewis, Clark and the men, each individual or group, being lulled into complacency by discovery, planning, construction, tonight's drink, trade and fornications, fail to recognize disaster on the horizon. In the western distance, the clouds have become solid and leaden, the wind has freshened, becoming gusty, the temperature and barometer drop in unison. The scout/hunters are the first of the groups to recognize the threat. They both independently raise the faces to the wind, sniff the air and sense the wind, temperature and humidity change. They both, unaware of the other, turn back toward the encampment.

Lt. Clark, while inventorying stores is the first to read the barometer nailed to an inside wall of the keelboat, 29.89" of mercury and falling. He looks out at the sky. An hour later, the barometer reads 29.78". The temperature is now 28 degrees Fahrenheit. The temperature has actually, risen in the past hour! A warmer, southerly flow is about to collide with a cold, northern low – heavy snow.

Drouillard and Braxton, the scout/hunters report back to camp just as the first snow begins to fall, then steadily. At first, work continues unabated, then, as the inches multiple upon one another, work slowly but conclusively ceases. By late afternoon, more than a foot of wet, heavy snow covers the earth, the wind shifts to a westerly, the snow to horizontal. Tents are hastily repositioned behind half-constructed, yet protective cabins, any remaining dry wood is scavenged and heaped into large fires. Everyone in the Corps layers for weather and prepares the evening's meal along with the next day's rations as well. A fierce storm descends upon the great westerly bend on the Missouri River and the encamped Corps of Discovery.

For three days and three nights the storm rages upon the prairie. Clark's carefully planned construction site is buried under feet of wet snow burnished by the winds into high, crusted drifts. Unprepared for such a calamity, the men stay huddled in small groups, shivering while sparingly nibbling their pre-cooked rations and sucking on snow. Then, as quickly as it arrived, the storm dissipates, the winds abate and the sun returns not unlike Penelope returning to the world of men from Hades and the Underworld.

Seaman is the first to escape a would-be frozen tomb. He senses movement above. He digs and sniffs, then digs some more. After only a short time, Seaman leaps out of the drift bank and into the open. Seaman catches the unsuspecting, foraging Hidatsa by surprise. Unlike their Lakota brothers to the south, this is the Hidatsa's first sight of Lewis' huge, black, bear-like Labrador dog. The Hidatsa talk excitedly among themselves realizing now that they may not be foraging dead white men's belongings, rather in a position to either kill the interlopers one by one as they emerge, or to provide helpful assistance to Lewis and his men as they begin to extract themselves from the snow. A monumental decision is thrust upon Buffalo Mane.

Buffalo Mane, being a man of peace, is not tempted by or swayed into a massacre of white men. The Hidatsa choose to assist the men of the Corps of Discovery survive the first snow of winter upon the plains.

Unbeknownst to him, Buffalo Mane's humanitarian gesture will ultimately lead to the death and disappearance of his tribe within two generations.

With harvest baskets, wooden paddles and bare hands, the Hidatsa village people excavate The Corps of Discovery. The cold, wet men are offered pemican, dried fruit and hot pumpkin soup as they emerge from their snowy caverns. Both parties suddenly begin to view one another differently; the Hidatsa seem more "human" to the white and the whites in their venerability, seem less threatening to the Hidatsa. Unfortunate however, this newly created bond will become a conduit of disease, abuse and virtual ethnic annihilation of the tribe.

Lewis pens.

December 10, 1804

A winter storm descended upon the area with such fury we were neither prepared or fared well. Were it not for the Hidatsa village effort, we would have surely perished from suffocation, cold or hunger. These people seem almost human. Although the heathen do display a certain level of organization, they do not rise to the level of western societal sophistication.

Even as Lewis closes the cover of his diary, the clock has begun to tick on the doomed Hidatsa. Within two decades, Buffalo Mane's people will near the brink of extinction.

Soon after the blizzard, both Lewis and Clark are anxious to continue talks with the Hidatsa and complete camp construction respectively. Lewis wishes to engage the big Frenchman and his Shoshoni child bride as interpreters and guides in the spring. A Shoshoni member of the Corps would be a most invaluable asset. He also wishes to somehow introduce his fossil find in a child's game of "show and tell", hopeful that either the Mandan or Hidatsa may also reveal long hidden artifacts in their possession. Clark, on the other hand, ever dutiful, hurries to complete his winter quarters plan and construction before the next winter storm and so that he may revisit and revise the many maps made during from Camp Du Bois to the Mandan villages, a formidable task.

Knows All has a foreboding dream; Hidatsa warriors falling from the sky, but without the bow, the arrow, lance or knife. They have not died in skirmish with the Lakota or Pawnee, yet they are dead. The wives and children of the warriors do not wail, scar themselves or shed tears of grief, for they are rolled up in blankets and dead also. Still the horses, and dogs, they live and wander about the village.

Knows All had dreamed the death of his people, yet he does not know when or why.

Perhaps The Original People have turned their backs to The Lone One? Perhaps The Lone One has removed himself from their presence? He cannot pray to the ancestors, there is no Aurora tonight. The dream leaves Knows All shaken and wet with sweat. He must consult the spirits.

EPILOGUE

As I noted in the Forward, it should be self-evident how the historical individuals and composite characters in this story each played a role in the early trajectory of "our" North American history. Unrelated to and separated by; race, culture and/or geography, each player makes his/her mark on this history. Governor for Life Louverture lit the match which started a conflagration ultimately extinguishing French colonialism, establishing independence and majority rule. F.B. Marbois is woven into the tapestry of French history; the late Bourbon, The Revolution, the Napoleonic era and then again in the Restoration of the monarchy. Speaking of the Napoleonic Era, our good General Napoleon, soon to be self-anointed Emperor of France, sells for cash money half a continent which he neither owns nor controls. With *huzpah* like that, Napoleon would have, without doubt, done well in the .Com Era on Wall Street. Jefferson, well, Jefferson is Jefferson, a giant of a man in intellect and will, yet as we all know, nonetheless a man. Before ultimately taking his own life (or the victim of a very cold case murder) Meriwether Lewis literally mapped the nation which we know today. And Sacagawea, she, as a trafficked teen-mother demonstrated the perseverance characteristic of indigenous peoples and the strength of her sex.

I have purposely used some generalizations but in these, there are to be found many defining traits.

I seek neither to beatify nor belittle any person or group rather recognize all as building blocks of this nation.

HISTORICAL CHARACTERS

1) Francois D.T. Louverture – The first Governor for Life of the island of Hispanola (Haiti/Dominican Republic) dies in a French prison in 1802.

2) Francois Barbe Marbois – Served his extraordinarily long life in successive French governments; Bourbon Louis XVI, Revolutionary France, Napoleonic French Empire as well as the Restoration and Louis XVIII.

3) Captain Meriwether Lewis – Tidewater gentry, Virginia militia, secretary to the President, Commander of the Corps of Discovery. Depressive suicide or murder victim 1809.

4) Seaman – Lewis' Labrador dog.

5) William Clark – Tidewater gentry, Virginia militia, plantation owner, slave owner, Second in Command Corps of Discovery, Superintendent of Indian Affairs Missouri, Governor of Missouri. Dies 1838.

6) Sacagawea – Shoshoni captive of the Sioux, wafered to Frenchtrapper Clarbonneau, teen mother, guide/interpreter to the Corps of Discovery. Probable death 1812, possible death 1884.

7) Sergeant Charles Floyd – Corps of Discovery. Only man to die on the Louisiana Purchase/Corps of Discovery expedition in 1803. Buried Floyd's Bluff Iowa.

8) Sergeant John Ordway – Senior NCO Corps of Discovery. Regular U.S. Army, 1st Inf. Div.

9) York – Clark's negro man servant. Son of Old York and Rose. Born 1770. Skilled man on the expedition but by correspondence is known to have remained enslaved to Clark as late as 1819. * Apparently Lewis and Clark never did have that conversation about the Rights of Man!

10) Composite characters include but are not limited to; Inspector Forneau, Professor DeBois, Oto-Missouri, Sioux, and Mandan Native Americans, Corporal Bratton and other men of the Corps.